THE SOMALI DECEPTION

EPISODE I

Daniel Arthur Smith

The Somali Deception Episode I
Copyright © 2010-14 Daniel Arthur Smith
All rights reserved Holt Smith ltd
Second Edition
Cover Design and Formatting by Daniel Arthur Smith
Edited by Crystal Watanabe

Published by Holt Smith Limited
ISBN: 0988649330
ISBN-13: 978-0-9886493-3-0

Also Written by Daniel Arthur Smith

The Cameron Kincaid Adventures
The Cathari Treasure
The Somali Deception

The Literary Fiction Series
The Potter's Daughter
Opening Day: A Short Story

The Horror Series
Agroland

~*~

For Susan, Tristan, & Oliver, as all things are.
&
To all of the others that choose to use crayons to color
their rainbows.

~*~

.

EPISODE I

CHAPTER 1
SEYCHELLES TUESDAY
02:35 HOURS SCT

Christine woke to yells from the decks above. She slid her hand over to the still warm spot where Nikos had been sleeping and then began to raise herself. Wine and darkness pulled her back toward her pillow. She pressed her hand down hard on the mattress to steady the spinning bed and then pushed herself up further.

Softly she spoke to the darkness, "Nikos."

No one answered.

Again she said his name, this time louder, "Nikos."

The yacht was still.

Christine shifted to the side of the bed, dizzy from the subtle movement. The shouts above were scattered, unclear, and the voices strange.

The yelling stopped. The darkness, stillness, and silence enveloped her. The cabin air became thick and the remnants of the wine again pulled at her forehead, down her neck, into her stomach. The blood rushing through her core caused her to gag.

The handle of the cabin hatch came to life suddenly.

The stillness broken, her chest went tight. Breathing ceased, her lungs held hostage by muscles squeezing deep into her neck, chin, jaw. She felt the sensation of falling back and away, the urge to vomit, to escape, and then, a rapid eruption of adrenalin. Christine's body was overcome in a wave of forced compensation as all of her muscles released. Her breathing returned, faster than measure. Clenching the edge of the blanket, she pulled the velour in tight to her lips to stifle the sound of her low feeble sobs. Hard forced clicks from the latch filled the stateroom. Though the cabin was a shroud of black, Christine set her eyes wide in the direction of the imminent intrusion. Futilely, she began to back pedal against the slick silk sheets, sinking deep into the cushioned headboard.

Across the room, metal slapped against metal, repeated two, three times, and then abruptly stopped.

The hatch was locked yet the chemicals flooding her system offered no quarter. The intrusion was imminent. Muffled whimpers continued to betray Christine despite her efforts to shield her mouth, and the hot rapid breaths that coursed through her nose were thunderous in the silence of the cabin. Throughout her chest and throat, her mouth and nose, the sensation of more breath out than in, each gasp a magnitude of terror.

A volley of gunshots interrupted the silence, followed by a barking shout.

She broke down what was happening on the yacht into a series of actions spaced eternally apart. Each silent divide an escalating stretch of anxiety towering over the last.

Nikos had assured her that to anchor on the far side of Curieuse was safe. The beach was in view from the deck, a far swim at most in the warm azure sea, and they were so close to Mahé, a mere forty kilometers to Victoria.

From the edge of the room, she heard the smooth metallic grate of a key being slid into the hatch and then tumblers falling into place.

Christine wanted Nikos to be the one turning the key.

With a final click of the lock, the hatch smoothly fell ajar. A seam of light sliced through the cabin. Christine winced. Her eyes tightened, opened, then tightened again.

She was initially blinded by the glare from the hall, then her eyes adjusted to the form before her.

The open hatch was cut with the backlit silhouette of a towering man, his arms contoured, his head a smooth sphere. Two other men of smaller stature stood behind the first. Christine focused her green eyes onto one of the sconces lining the hall. The two men behind the silhouette were both dark Africans, one in a light soiled t-shirt, the other was shirtless, each with a Kalashnikov strapped over a thin shoulder.

The tall bald man hunched down into the stateroom. She watched the outline of the fingers of one hand spread wide then slip away to the dark inside edge of the doorway. The man's arm snaked up until he found the switch he was seeking. With a click, the sconces fastened above each side of the master bed illuminated the cabin with an amber glow. The man, another African, darker than the others, surveyed the room. His eyes scanned the dressers snug under the side berth and cabin windows. He inspected the closet doors and the opened entrance to the head. Not once did the bald giant's eyes focus on the near naked woman, a model by trade, peering at him from the master bed.

With a wave of his hand, the tall man gestured the two gaunt Kalashnikov bearers into the stateroom. The men reached down between them and from the floor lifted a shirtless Caucasian. The two men effortlessly dragged the unconscious man toward Christine.

As the men moved closer, Christine's feeble whimpers rose to convulsive sobs. Frozen against the cushioned headboard, her eyes began to flood.

The bright green of her eyes glazed over with the well of tears and her head and neck pressed back so tightly against the headboard that with each thudding pulse, the thundering rush of blood pained the base of her skull.

3

The two men carried the ragdoll of a man over to the bed and then with a dip and a lift, they heaved the lifeless figure next to her. Her eyes shot to the bloody face. The beaten man was Nikos. Her heart swelled, throbbing against her lungs, preventing air from getting in.

Nikos looked dead.

Christine dropped her hand to Nikos' forehead to move his blood-matted hair away from his face. She ran her thumb over his brow, first smearing, and then clearing blood away from the small cut near his eye.

Nikos coughed weakly. He was alive. She was able to take in a deep breath.

She caressed Nikos' cheek, "It's going to be okay, Nikos." She was unsure if more than a soft wisp had escaped her dry throat.

Nikos' eyes were already swelling shut and he was having trouble opening them. His jaw opened and then closed, only a faint breath escaped.

She exerted more effort into her voice, "Shhh, don't try to talk."

The hatch slammed shut, followed by the metal clack of the bolt. Christine raised her head, her eyes frantically darting to the hatch and then searching the rest of the still lit room.

Christine and Nikos were alone.

CHAPTER 2
UPPER WEST SIDE, NEW YORK

Cameron reached deep into the loose right pocket of his slacks for the key to Le Dragon Vert. He usually threw jeans on after taping down in Chelsea, but tonight he didn't bother. He walked alone along West Eighty-first Street. This time of night, the sidewalks of the Upper West Side were near empty. To his right, the massive Hayden Sphere glowed soft indigo in the six-story glass cube Rose Center, a nightlight for the wealthy residents of Central Park West. Cameron sucked in the fragrance of the daffodils carpeting the small Roosevelt Park bordering the museum. Two taxis drove under the traffic light from the Central Park crosstown entrance. Cameron waited for the yellow cabs to pass and then jaywalked across Eighty-first Street to his restaurant.

Cameron slipped his key into the front door of Le Dragon Vert, closed for the evening an hour before. He skipped down the three steps from the vestibule into the amber lit lounge, his attention immediately drawn to the bar. The dark oak bar jutted into the edge of the lounge then ran the length of the tunneled hallway that led to the dining room. Midway down the dimly lit tunnel two men, one thin, one stout, sat on leather seats conversing softly. The wide man, his back to Cameron, concealed all but the shoulder of the second. Without seeing their faces, Cameron recognized them both. His mentor and partner in the restaurant, Claude Rambeaux, owned the thin shoulder, and the girth and thick black hair of the other belonged to his friend Pepe Laroque, visiting New York from Montreal.

Cameron approached his two friends, both former members of the same super elite Legionnaire regiment that he himself had belonged to years before. He placed a hand on each of their shoulders. "I see you found the Ardbeg single malt," he said.

"Claude says you charge seventy dollars for a drink of this," said Pepe.

Cameron curled his lip, "It is thirty years old. Everything okay? I wasn't expecting you."

Since Pepe had been in the French Foreign Legion with Cameron and Claude, he was far more than just a dear old friend. Cameron knew Pepe as a man would know a brother. Pepe was never too far from a glass of wine or brandy. Hard liquor, however, was not his drink of choice. On the bar was a bottle of whiskey and three glasses.

Claude picked up the rock glass he had set aside for Cameron and then poured two fingers of the single malt.

"Have a seat," said Claude. "I expected you back from the studio a few hours ago."

Cameron reached behind Claude for a stool and then pulled the seat to where he stood. "I took my competitor out for a drink. Life on the soundstage isn't what he thought it would be."

Claude handed Cameron the half filled glass. Cameron held it up, and the others followed suit.

"Vive la Légion," said Cameron.

In unison, Pepe and Claude responded, "The Legion is our strength."

"That is good," said Cameron, after sampling the single malt. "So I take it there's no funeral. What are we celebrating?"

"No celebration, I'm afraid," said Pepe. He placed his palm on his forehead and held his hand there, letting his eyes slowly close. After a pause, he wiped his hand across his brow, let his eyes rest open, and looked into his palm. "The whiskey heats you up," he said, and then feigned a smile.

Pepe's smile was that of a cherub, high into his puffed cheeks. Still, Cameron suspected bad news. "What is it, Pepe?"

"Tell him," said Claude, "Go ahead."

"Remember Langdon?" asked Pepe.

"Sergeant Langdon? Yeah, I remember him."

"Well, he's Adjutant-Chef Langdon now."

Adjutant-Chef was the equivalent of Lieutenant in the Legion and essentially a sub-officer. "Huh, the world keeps changing," said Cameron. "What about him?"

"He called me this morning. One of Langdon's men is the IMB liaison."

"The International Marine Bureau," said Claude. Cameron nodded.

Pepe nodded his head and then said, "Langdon gets all the reports from the IMB piracy reporting center in Kuala Lumpur. Five days ago the Kalinihta, a forty-five meter yacht, sailed from the Seychelles at 0300 local time without notifying anyone. Kuala Lumpur is tracking the yacht. Her heading appears to be south of Mogadishu."

"What," said Cameron. "So you're saying the yacht was taken?"

"The reporting center is not sure, they cannot make contact."

"I don't understand," said Claude.

"The owner of the Kalinihta hasn't reported her missing."

"If she's not missing, why are they watching the yacht from Kuala Lumpur?" asked Claude.

"Because of who owns the yacht," said Cameron.

"Somebody important owns the Kalinihta."

"Exactly," said Pepe. "The Kalinihta is owned by Demetrius Stratos, the Greek shipping magnate. The GPS on the Kalinihta links directly to the IMB. They monitor its movements and the Captain checks in regularly. If the yacht moves a meter, they know."

"Sounds like the Somali," said Cameron. "Though I didn't think the pirates went that far out." He sipped from his rock glass. "I'm sure Stratos is keeping it quiet to deal with it himself."

Pepe nodded and made a soft grunting sound in the back of his throat.

"Why did they notify Langdon?" asked Claude. "Is the Kalinihta flying a French flag? I know our boys have zero tolerance for French hostages."

"The flag is Panamanian. Demetrius has a son, Nikos. He was last seen on the yacht the day before with a model he has been dating. She is the French citizen."

"So the IMB called Langdon," said Cameron. "I'm missing something. Why did Langdon call you?"

Pepe's eyes appeared sunken, and from beneath his meaty brow he peered deeply at Cameron. The corners of his mouth went taut into his full cheeks.

"What?" asked Cameron.

"Cameron," said Pepe. "The model is Christine."

"Pepe," said Claude. "Your sister Christine?"

"She was with Nikos on the yacht," said Pepe.

"Are you sure? " asked Cameron. He leaned forward to set his whiskey on the bar. "I mean, she takes off all the time. Are you sure she was on the yacht?"

"I'm sure," said Pepe. "I called her roommate in Paris. She told me Christine had flown to the Seychelles with Nikos and that she has not heard from her since."

Cameron pushed his hands into his knees and tilted his head back to face the ceiling. His mind flooded with youthful images of a smiling, laughing Christine.

"And Langdon," said Claude. "What's he going to do,

take a team to board the yacht?"

Pepe shook his head, "No, until the Kalinihta is reported hijacked there is nothing he can do."

"I see," said Claude.

"Hostages are held on the average of forty-five days before a ransom is paid," said Pepe. "I don't think it would take Stratos that long to come up with the money. If he sends in his own team, who knows."

Cameron brought his head back forward and straightened his neck. He lifted his hand from his knee and firmly gripped Pepe's shoulder. "So when do we leave?"

Pepe grinned. He reached across his chest, patted Cameron's hand, and then from his jacket he brought out a pair of heavy rimmed black glasses and a folded sheet of paper. He slipped on the glasses, opened the sheet, and leaned his head forward, tilting the paper toward the dim light behind the bar.

"We fly out of JFK at 7:50pm for Nairobi," said Pepe. He lowered the paper and peered over the rim of his glasses toward Cameron. "We layover in London for a few hours. In all, it should take about twenty."

"That will give us time to make some calls," said Cameron. "I take it you already contacted Alastair?"

"I have, his people will meet us in Nairobi and take us to meet him at the eco-lodge."

"Eco-lodge, I like that." Cameron's right hand was still on Pepe's shoulder and the other was retrieving his whiskey from the bar. "Claude, I'll need you to—,"

"I know, don't worry," said Claude. "Just get Christine home safely."

Cameron lifted his glass into the air. "To Somalia via Kenya we go."

Pepe lifted his glass to the toast and then the three drank.

CHAPTER 3
ATLANTIC OCEAN

Cameron pulled the light blanket over his chin. This flight contrasted the countless missions he'd flown as a young Legionnaire. In the Legion, there were far more takeoffs than landings and never had a flight been this comfortable. Pepe had arranged sleeper service for the two of them. They were served a full dinner pre-flight at the JFK VIP lounge and then as soon as the Boeing 777 left the runway, the flight attendants started a turn down service. Next to each other in opposing directions, the back and front of their two sleeper seats reclined and lifted to create two-meter berths. A little tall for the mattress, Cameron was still able to relax, though sleep would not come easy. Cameron was well aware that on the other side of the divider, Pepe was reviewing the latest details of the hijacked yacht.

Six days had passed since the Kalinihta had been hijacked. The last GPS coordinates had put the Kalinihta, still not reported missing, near the small port city of Kismayu, 500 kilometers down the African coast from Mogadishu. Pepe had shared with Cameron what he'd learned from Langdon. On board the yacht were Christine,

Nikos Stratos, the captain, cook, three crewmen, and two other women, one a maid and the other a steward. The captain, Warren Lewis, was an older British man, well seasoned with a commercial background. The cook and two women were Greek, the steward the cook's girlfriend. Two of the crewmen were brothers from Genoa, Aberto and Donato Disota, and the third was a Seychellois, local to where the Kalinihta was anchored. Langdon had told Pepe that for a crew that size, the pirates would most likely ask for a million US dollars, expecting to get half.

Cameron had done some homework as well. Before leaving New York, he'd made some calls concerning Demetrius Stratos. As a civilian, a commando, and later as undercover ops, Cameron had come across men like Stratos, powerful men unabashed by their actions, men with egos that forbade them from receiving insult without swift response. Stratos would not turn his back on his son and he was not the kind of man that would easily pay a ransom. For men with the power Stratos possessed, there was an alternative resolve. Cameron and Pepe were undoubtedly not the only former soldiers on their way to Somalia.

The top of the cabin reflected the pale blue glow of Pepe's MacBook Pro. Cameron could visualize the drill. Pepe was checking the coordinates of Kismayu and key points in the vicinity against Google Earth or some other plat map. Christine was Pepe's little sister. Pepe spoke of her as if she were tough, but Cameron thought differently; they'd had something years ago. The tough exterior was an act, Christine was softer than Pepe wanted to admit. Sophisticated and well traveled, to call Christine fragile would be a mistake, yet a week as a hostage would be enough to break most anybody.

Cameron took a breath in through his nose as he again processed the thought of Christine being held hostage. He drew a mental picture of Christine on the yacht. The image of Christine was of her the last time they spoke. That would not be right though; almost ten years had passed since the last time Cameron had seen her in person, and though she was still beautiful, she had matured, lost the girlish features. Cameron thought Christine would more closely resemble the woman she portrayed in the ads, a visage combined from cosmetics and Photoshop.

The beauty was real though.

What Cameron and Christine had together had been real.

Cameron told himself that Christine was the one that got away. He'd let her slip away. They had met in Paris when Christine first began modeling. Pepe had introduced them over lunch and, in fear of insulting or hurting Pepe, the two began seeing each other in secrecy. When Pepe did finally confront them, he was not angry. Pepe gave them his blessing and told them that nothing would please him more than seeing his brother-in-arms marry his sister.

That probably would have happened had Cameron and Christine chosen different careers. They spent too much time apart, each with jobs that took them far around the world, Christine to the fashion meccas of the wealthiest countries and Cameron to the hot spots of the poorest. As Cameron's work began to involve deep cover operations, the time they spent apart grew from weeks to months. The missions Cameron became involved in were dangerous and with each, the risk of fatality increased. Looking back, Cameron could see that Christine would have understood, would have waited for him. At the time, Cameron thought it best to let Christine go on without him.

Cameron had more than once imagined a different life where he and Christine had gone farther together. There were children that looked like them with chestnut hair, his chin, her cheeks, and her green eyes below his brow. Cameron always imagined them all happy.

Yet thinking about a past that had never occurred and a present that did not exist was futile, so when nostalgic thoughts arose, melancholy or pleasant, they were expeditiously warded away. Chased away as other futile thoughts were by simple sage advice that Claude had given Cameron years before. "Men like us," Claude had said, "should not tally regret."

Regardless of a past shared and unshared, Christine was in trouble and her rescue was up to Pepe and Cameron. A rescue from captors that did not know the mistake they were making by boarding the Kalinihta.

CHAPTER 4
LONDON HEATHROW AIRPORT

The flight attendant appeared no older than a teen. She leaned in toward Pepe, her shoulders tight, arms straight, and her hands pressed against her knees. She spoke softly, as though sharing a secret, her British accent both formal and kind, "Mister Laroque, when you and Mister Kincaid disembark, a London crewmember will be waiting outside the Jetway."

"Thank you, Rachelle. I appreciate your extra effort contacting Heathrow," he said.

"Nonsense, Mister Laroque, it is my pleasure. Can I get you anything before we land?"

"No, I'm quite fine."

Rachelle gave Pepe a departing smile and then shifted her focus to Cameron. "Can I get you anything, Mister Kincaid?"

"I'm quite fine as well. Thank you," said Cameron.

"Very well gentlemen, please prepare for landing."

Cameron and Pepe gave Rachelle a friendly nod and then locked eyes with each other.

"Cameron," said Pepe.

"I know," said Cameron.

Cameron peered out the window beyond Pepe. White billows enveloped the large jet airliner as she fell through the clouds.

Rachelle opened a cabinet near the ceiling and pressed the first of five buttons that crossed the face of a black metal console. In the next cabin, a voice as formal and kind as Rachelle's relayed an automated message asking passengers to please check that their tray tops were up, their seatbelts were fastened, and that their seatbacks were in an upright position.

Outside the window, white wisps of moisture revealed first hazily, then concisely, the details of soft green terra firma fields, roofs of row houses, and then lastly, the myriad of utility sheds and parcel depots skirting London Heathrow.

A muffled thump rose from the deck as the Boeing triple seven kissed the Heathrow tarmac coupled with the immediate roar of the engine's reverse thrust. The travelers lurched forward and then eased back, the engines lulled, and applause filled the coach cabin. Rather than take part in the transatlantic landing ritual, Cameron gathered his gear. Time in London was to be short, hurried by the departure of the Kenyan flight. Pepe had gathered his gear together moments before and was now bent slightly forward at the waist, his feet and knees together, eyes open, chin to chest, elbows tight into his sides and his fingers spread wide from his extended hands. Cameron recognized the posture. Pepe held the posture paratroopers assumed before leaving a plane. Pepe was in jump position and prepared to launch himself when the cabin door opened.

Pepe did not have long to wait.

As the jet taxied toward the terminal, Rachelle walked passed Pepe and into the small service area demarcating the sleeper section of the cabin from coach. She pulled the privacy curtain from the side of the fuselage to clear the exit and then waited in front of the hatch. The jet stopped, bumped forward, and then began moving again under the power of a small tow vehicle below.

Cameron could see from his seat the glass Jet Bridge closing in on the side of the Boeing.

The two men stood and approached Rachelle. She was awkwardly hunched forward, peering up through the hatch window, coordinating with the Jet Bridge operator by means of a black telephone receiver jacked into the side of the cabin door. Rachelle turned and smiled widely at Pepe and Cameron, flirtatiously raising her eyebrows as they approached. The men appreciated they were to have remained seated. She merely continued to respond to the operator with monosyllabic statements, "Clear... Clear... Five and... Clear..."

With a subtle jolt, the Jet Bridge fastened to the side of the fuselage. Rachelle seated the receiver and pulled the latch to release the cabin door.

"Welcome to Heathrow, gentlemen," said Rachelle, pulling the door clear for Pepe and Cameron to exit.

"Merci," said Pepe.

A series of faint bells rang through the cabin. Passengers began to lift themselves from their seats and gather their carry on luggage from the overhead compartments.

"Ms. Conroy will be to the right of the Jet Bridge," said Rachelle. Her voice raised an octave, "Thank you for flying."

This time Cameron responded, "Thank you." Then he shot out the hatch to catch up with Pepe, who was already halfway up the glass corridor.

~*~

Ms. Conroy, a petite woman with blonde hair fashioned no hassle pixie style, briskly walked toward Cameron and Pepe from the entrance of the Jet Bridge. She wore a Heathrow blazer and on her arm, a clipboard filled with sheets of itinerary that had been shuffled and flipped through a number of times before her latest wards had arrived. In her other hand, she held a two-way mobile.

"Good morning, Mister Laroque, Mister Kincaid. My name is Ms. Conroy. Welcome to London Heathrow. If you could follow me, please."

Before Pepe or Cameron could respond to Ms. Conroy's greeting, she had spun around back toward the Jet Bridge entrance and in two steps was leaning on a side door that led down to the tarmac. In the same motion, she lifted the two-way and spoke into the device, "I have them with me. Side alpha-2, word of the hour," Ms. Conroy paused and tilted her wrist to see her watch, "Giraffe." The magnetic lock buzzed and Ms. Conroy pushed the large metal and glass door open, giving her small frame the appearance of great might. The moist air surged in thick from the rainy grey world outside of the enclosed terminal. Pepe and Cameron had to pick up their step to keep in stride with Ms. Conroy as she shot down the steps and onto the wet tarmac toward a waiting van directly below the Jet Bridge. She jerked the side door of the van open with the hand holding the two-way and then stepped back.

"Please step aboard, gentlemen," said Ms. Conroy, an expedient machine a moment before, now poised and courteous. Cameron and Pepe climbed into the van, each nodding to the smiling young woman. She threw the door closed once they were clear and then hurled herself into the front passenger seat. Cameron raised a brow to Pepe and both were rocked back into their seats as the van accelerated away from the Jet Bridge out onto the tarmac across a road designated only by two white painted lines. The van shifted to either side, negotiating the course, the large single wiper slicing the gathering water from the windscreen, the onboard radio chirping porter information across the complex. Ms. Conroy was on her two-way as well, a different channel, flipping through her clipboard and marking the lists of flights with notations of names, checkmarks, and times with numerous circles.

Cameron and Pepe had spent years of their lives on tarmacs and found the ride familiar. While thousands of patrons roamed the terminals, the hidden underbelly of the great animal that was London Heathrow functioned as a giant organism. The van a corpuscle surging through with momentum under the wings of jets, around trains of baggage carts, petrol trucks, and dozens of other vehicles that were all part of the Heathrow eco, all moving to a breakneck choreography to accommodate the two hundred thousand people being served each day.

"Mister Laroque," said Ms. Conroy. "As London is not your final destination, arrangements have been made for Mister Kincaid and yourself. This will only take a moment. Please have your passports ready."

The van cleared the back of a petrol truck and then spun a 180-degree turn, pulling up next to a small white concrete block building. Ms. Conroy threw open her door and in a single borderline acrobatic maneuver, swung out and slid the side panel of the van open.

Every time Ms. Conroy spouted an order, her voice would raise to a polite pitch. "This way, please," she said, again marching away before Cameron or Pepe could respond.

The white building was as Spartan on the inside as out, consisting of four walls and a glassed-in customs agent on one end. To the side, a small room divider lead away from the customs desk, masking a table. Cameron and Pepe followed Ms. Conroy through the door and waited for her cue. "Wait here, please," said Ms. Conroy. She approached the agent then said something the two men could not hear that prompted him to nod his head.

"Very good, then," said Ms. Conroy. "Mister Laroque, you first please, and then Mister Kincaid."

Pepe walked the four steps to the glass. The agent held up his open hand and said nothing. Pepe offered his French passport. The agent placed the passport on his desk. He did not scan the passport or even bother to look at the picture. He opened the passport to the middle and then, finding the pages full, flipped until he found a blank. With a thud, he stamped the ID, then handed the passport back. Cameron stepped forward and the process was repeated. Before Cameron had his passport back in his hands, Ms. Conroy was at the door.

Ms. Conroy led Pepe and Cameron to the rear of a black Bentley that had driven up to the door of the discrete Customs building. Seeing his passengers exit, the driver stepped out of the black limo and opened the rear door. Ms. Conroy handed Pepe a packet. "The tickets for your next leg are here. Instructions with the flight time and where to enter the airport are included." Ms. Conroy smirked, "Please be prompt. The driver your friend has arranged also has these instructions, so you should be fine. You will not need to go through Customs again as you have never left the airport. Your friend felt the formality of the stamp beneficial in the event your stay is prolonged. One never knows."

"One never knows, Ms. Conroy. Merci," said Pepe.

"Good day, then," said Ms. Conroy, flashing a broad smile. Then, in her manner, she briskly marched back to the van, already back to chatting into her two-way and flipping through reshuffled itineraries.

CHAPTER 5
LONDON MAYFAIR

Cameron rubbed his temples. He peered up and out the window of the Bentley to the London sky, and then over to Pepe.

"The man we are going to meet here in London is a Somali expat," said Pepe. "I was made aware of him by a contact back in Montreal."

"Did your contact mention how he knows this man?" asked Cameron.

"The man in Montreal said that he and the London man used to be fishermen. I was told we would find him at The May Fair Hotel."

"You sure? A lot of workers move in and out of that place."

"I am sure. I was told he does not work there," Pepe threw an eye to Cameron. "He lives there."

Cameron arched a brow, "He lives at The May Fair?"

Pepe nodded, "He used to be a fisherman. We are not all what we were."

The driver glanced into the rearview mirror, "Excuse me, gentlemen. We will be at The May Fair Hotel shortly."

Pepe gazed far out into the grey day. "This area of the city is nice. What is that large building in the center of the park over there? It is very familiar. Is that a museum?"

"In a manner of speaking, sir," said the driver. "That would be Buckingham Palace, home to her majesty the Queen. The May Fair Hotel is around the next corner."

Pepe tilted his head forward for a better view, "Very nice, eh Cameron?"

"The May Fair Hotel is a five star hotel, one of the finest in the world," said Cameron. "It appears our friend is living rather upscale."

"My contact did mention that the man we are meeting with is a bit of an entrepreneur," said Pepe.

~*~

A porter opened the rear door of the Bentley and Cameron began to exit from the car.

"Sir," said the driver. He was looking in the rearview mirror again, this time directly at Pepe. Cameron elbowed Pepe's upper arm.

"Oh, excusez-moi," said Pepe, putting his hand into his jacket.

"Oh, no sir," said the driver. "That is not necessary." Pepe stopped reaching for a tip and waited. From over the top of the seat, the driver presented Pepe with what appeared to be a small black key fob.

"Please take this," said the driver. He tapped the flat panel screen on his console. "I will know when you are approaching the lobby and are ready to be taken back to the airport. You can tap and hold the button as well."

"Tap and hold?"

"Yes, sir," said the driver. "Tap and hold."

"All right then," said Pepe. "We will only be a short while."

The driver nodded. Pepe nodded back, uncertain what to say next.

"Let's go," said Cameron. He shifted out of the Bentley toward the waiting doorman.

"Right," said Pepe, and then he scooted out behind his friend.

The few short steps from the Bentley to the lobby were a contrast of worlds. Cameron and Pepe entered the lobby below a ruby-laden Baccarat chandelier and surrounding them were eclectic Russian, Thai, and Vietnamese objects d'art, the finest London had to offer. Cameron immediately approached the Clef d'Or concierge, the two crossed golden keys on the man's lapel shimmering in the lobby light.

The concierge clasped his hands together when he saw Cameron. "We are graced by the Dragon Chef. Mister Kincaid, we did not know you were arriving today," said the concierge.

"My visit was not announced," said Cameron.

"We have missed you since your visit with our last Chef. I will call the restaurant at once and let them know you are here. Our new Chef is out, yet I believe she will be back from the market shortly."

Cameron lifted his hands, "I would rather you did not. Though I would love to hold court with the Queen of Eastern European Cuisine, I am actually here on different business."

The concierge let his face go blank. "Discretion is my business."

"Thank you. My friend and I are here to see someone who is living at The May Fair."

"I see. A private audience with the Dragon Chef and..." the concierge lifted his gaze to Pepe.

"My sommelier," said Cameron.

The concierge drew his brows together, "And sommelier. Of course, what is food without wine? And who is it that we are going to see?"

Pepe leaned into the concierge and whispered into his ear. The concierge's eyes grew wide. Cameron took note.

"Discretion," said Cameron softly.

The concierge composed himself. He reached below his counter to prepare a magnetic keycard. "The guest you wish to see is staying in one of our signature suites, the Amber. The suite is on the fourth floor, this key will take you there, and I will ring them of your arrival."

"Thank you," said Cameron. "We are expected under the name of—,"

"D'artagnan," said Pepe.

The concierge swallowed hard, "D'artagnan, yes, of course," he recovered a cordial smile. "Discretion."

Cameron did not directly look back at the concierge, though through his trained attention to peripheral detail, he noticed the concierge's friendly and genteel gaze shift to a leer as the two made their way to the lift.

"Who is this guy we're going to see?" asked Cameron under his breath. "What is his name?"

Pepe also had metered the concierge's response, "I do not know who this guy is. The name I was given was Smith, Ibrahim Smith. The concierge though, he was very disturbed."

Cameron curled his lip, "Of course he would be a Smith."

CHAPTER 6
THE MAY FAIR HOTEL, LONDON
MAYFAIR

Cameron and Pepe entered the lift and then inserted the keycard into the slot next to the button designating the fourth floor. The cabin rapidly ascended to the luxury level. Immediately they saw which door led to the Amber suite. Halfway down the corridor, a massive bodyguard stood sentinel outside of a doorway, his eyes glazed and fixed on the wall to his front. Cameron and Pepe approached the door. The large man, a giant, did not shift his gaze or girth. The door opened without Cameron or Pepe having to announce their presence. Shadowing the inner frame of the door was another titan as large and solid as the sentinel, though this second guard was animate. He gestured the two men into the suite where, by the door, they saw a chair and a table topped with a monitor displaying the hallway. Behind them, they heard the door close and then the clicks of several locks engaging on top and bottom. The titan then strode past them. "This way," he said, and led them into the heart of the beige and brown apartment sized suite.

As the name of the room implied, amber was the

predominant theme. The numerous objects d'art in the room were all made of amber, as were the many lamps. The centerpiece of the room was a large L-shaped sofa upholstered with amber hued crushed velvet. In the center of the sofa, so as to treat the room as his dominion, sat a well-groomed dark African man. The man was not young, though he appeared in fine health. The man's suit was impeccable, and certainly, Savile Row tailored. The man, undoubtedly Mister Smith, was watching a football match on the 42-inch Bang & Olufsen plasma television centered on the wall. Mister Smith was indifferent to Cameron and Pepe entering the room. Pepe and Cameron stood silently and watched the match from the side of the sofa. One of the players kicked a far pass and a raucous noise shot from the stadium crowd through the many surround sound speakers hidden throughout the suite. Mister Smith flashed a glance at the large bodyguard still standing to the side of the two and then wagged a finger at the screen. The bodyguard held up the television remote.

"Just the volume," said Mister Smith, his voice deep and absolute. The volume went down. The man still made no eye contact with Cameron or Pepe. "Please, sit. I apologize. Like most men, sport takes me to my youth."

"I understand," said Pepe. He and Cameron sat on a small matching sofa perpendicular to Mister Smith.

"Our friend in Montreal believes I may be able to help you," said Mister Smith.

Pepe nodded, "I would like that. He said that you know Somalia, that you and he were fishermen."

Mister Smith chuckled. "Yes, that is true. All of us on the coast were fishermen once, when there were fish. Now I am a diplomat."

Pepe scanned the suite, "Our friend also said you were an entrepreneur. I see diplomacy has perks."

"Yes, perks. Can I get you anything?" Mister Smith raised his hand again to the bodyguard.

"No, thank you. We are really on a tight schedule,"

said Cameron. "I am sure you understand."

Mister Smith let his hand suspend for a long few seconds and then reached for a rock glass on the dark wooden table before him. He lifted the glass, relished a sip of the clear liquid inside, and then continued to speak, "Yes, you have a plane to catch. Listen, I am sorry I do not have any news for you."

Pepe dropped his head, "I see."

"I have made inquiries though, and I am sure I will have a name for you shortly. Give your number to my man. I could not hold this position without having a pulse on who is responsible for such actions."

"Thank you for your time," said Pepe, rising with Cameron from the small sofa.

"Do you need a driver or a pilot back to Heathrow?" asked Mister Smith "It is the least I can do. For now."

"No, we have a car waiting," said Cameron.

Mister Smith again wagged his finger toward the screen. The suite filled again with the sound of the football match. The bodyguard raised his arm toward a sidebar behind Cameron and Pepe. On the end, Pepe found May Fair Hotel stationary and pens. He wrote down a number where a message could be left then turned to tell Mister Smith, but Mister Smith was once again indifferent to their presence. The titan held his hand out and Pepe relinquished the number to him.

Cameron waited until the two were in the lift before he spoke. "Did you recognize him?"

"Even after all of these years, his face has not changed," said Pepe.

"I was thinking the same," said Cameron. "He calls himself a diplomat now."

Pepe pulled the key fob from his pocket that the driver had given him and then pressed the button. "He can call himself a diplomat all he wants, the man is still a warlord."

CHAPTER 7
THE MAY FAIR HOTEL, LONDON
MAYFAIR

The lift descended past the lobby down to a sublevel.

"I thought you tapped the button," said Pepe.

"I did," said Cameron. "We probably have to go to the bottom and work our way back up."

Cameron heard a slight grunt from Pepe. The meeting with Mister Smith had not been fruitful. A ping rang from the digital panel and the cabin doors opened to two dark African men, one attired in a brown suit, the other blue, both suits cheap. Though they were in a subterranean level, the man in the blue suit was wearing dark sunglasses.

"Please step out of the lift, gentlemen," said the man in the brown suit, gesturing toward an older model white Bentley parked behind him.

Cameron and Pepe shared a glance and a slight nod.

"I have been to this hotel several times and was unaware there was underground parking. I believe I will have to speak to the concierge," said Cameron.

"Apparently this level is invite only," said Pepe.

The brown suited man's eyebrows lifted, "If you

please."

"Why would we want to do that?" asked Cameron.

The man in the brown suit smiled widely then took a step back from the doorway. The man in the blue suit stepped back as well, then lifted the corner of his jacket to reveal a revolver.

"Please," said the man in the brown suit. "Our employer only asks for a moment of your time."

Cameron lifted his hands to the height of his chest and Pepe did the same. "Okay," said Cameron, "Since you said please."

"Invite only," said Pepe.

Cameron and Pepe eased from the lift toward the white Bentley, keeping their hands raised high. Leery of any sudden action, the two men in suits shadowed them from a wary distance on either side, careful not to step too close.

Now out in the open, Cameron could see down the row of parked cars in the garage. At the far end of the aisle, easing slowly into position, was the newer Bentley they had arrived in. Between Pepe's thumb and index finger, Cameron could see the key fob their driver had given them. Pepe was subtly holding the button down and though they were in a lower level, a level previously unknown to Cameron, the signal was strong enough to reach the driver, a man obviously of privileged information.

Cameron and Pepe stopped short of the vintage white Bentley.

"You know we are not getting into that car," said Cameron.

The men in the suits said nothing, and stopped as well, one at the rear of the Bentley, one at the front. The front door then opened and out stepped the Bentley's driver. The driver was also an African man and rather than acknowledge the two men standing with their hands raised, he disregarded them altogether, instead reaching for the handle of the rear door.

The white suit that exited the rear of the Bentley was

neither cheap nor small. Though an odd choice of color, the suit was another tailored on Savile Row, and as impeccable as the one Cameron and Pepe had seen upstairs moments ago. The bald giant towered high over Cameron and Pepe.

"Relax, gentleman," said the bald giant.

Cameron and Pepe eased their arms down. "I suppose you don't want to call attention to the cameras," said Cameron.

The tall man lifted his hand and twirled his finger in a circle, "The cameras went away when the elevator missed the lobby."

"I see," said Cameron. "So what do you want?"

"Me," said the tall man, his face not gathering expression, "I want nothing."

"Then why the detour?"

"The man I work for, now he wants something."

"Okay, now we are getting somewhere. What is it?"

"The two of you came here to visit a man, to ask questions. Is that so?"

"So what if it is?" asked Pepe.

The tall man fixed his eyes on Pepe, "My employer wishes for you to stop. What is the expression? You are sticking your nose where it does not belong. Into the business of others."

"And if we do not stop?" asked Pepe.

"First, we will harm your sister, Mister Laroque, then we will come for you."

Pepe spoke cool and slow, "It's a shame those cameras are not on."

"And why is that?" said the tall man, for the first time showing a sense of inquisitive interest. He tilted his head and focused a threatening leer toward Pepe.

In a fluid motion, rotund Pepe propelled himself up and threw his forehead toward the tall man while Cameron simultaneously pulled the chrome Magnum from inside the white belt of the tall man's suit. As Pepe fell back toward the ground, Cameron put a bullet through the forehead of the brown suit, then spun and put two scarlet holes into the head of the blue suited man. The blue suited man had drawn his revolver free from his waist, yet had not raised his weapon in time. Upon hearing the shots fired, the new Bentley squealed down the aisle toward them. When Cameron spun back around, Pepe already had the tall bald man pinned on the ground with his knee pressed against his chest. The tall man's African driver was standing beside the Bentley shaking, easing his hand toward his waist.

"Don't do it," said Cameron.

The driver then made a darting motion toward the grip of his gun only to find himself sliding back against the Bentley on a slick of his own blood. His fingers had not even made a firm grasp.

Pepe leaned in close to the tall man, "It's a shame those cameras are not on," said Pepe once again. "Because I have to let you live to deliver this message to your boss. Tell him, I am coming."

CHAPTER 8
JOMO KENYATTA INTERNATIONAL AIRPORT, NAIROBI

The fierce Nairobi heat blanketed the tarmac, penetrating the fuselage and enveloping Cameron and Pepe inside. The pilot had cut the air conditioner early, stifling the cabin. Cameron and Pepe took their duffels from the overhead and waited for the steward to open the hatch. The pungent evening air flooded the fuselage when the hatch swung open.

The jet had traversed from Heathrow, midway to the polar cap, down to this equatorial heat and was now parked away from the terminal. Cameron and Pepe followed the queue out of the hatch and onto the mobile Airstair that was raised to the door from the back of a small truck.

The balmy darkness hung snug over the tarmac. Porters in brown canvas vests pulled handcarts stacked with luggage and parcels to smaller single and double engine prop planes on either side of the passenger jet Cameron and Pepe were now exiting.

Between two tattered red velvet ropes leading out of the Jomo Kenyatta international terminal stood a small crowd, above them a large number two marked the entry to the customs desk. As passengers disembarked, the crowd began to thin. Drivers quickly came forward to take whatever luggage their employer or assigned businessmen held in their hands. Family members embraced those returning home and those visiting from as far away as Cambodia and Australia. Halfway down the Airstair, Cameron saw Alastair Main standing at the back of the group with a well-groomed dark haired man.

Alastair may as well have walked off the cover of National Geographic. Alastair's hands were at his hips, his elbows wide akimbo, his chin high, and his yellow mane glowed bright against the backlit tarmac. Alastair threw a nod to Cameron and Pepe and then raised his hands out high into the air as he began to saunter toward them.

Alastair was a Brit, more so a colonial, though he despised the term, as he was born and raised in Kenya. He had served with Cameron and Pepe in the Legion and to them he was a brother.

When Alastair reached Pepe, he threw his arms around him and pulled him tight. Pepe kissed each of Alastair's cheeks.

Alastair threw a firm grip onto each of Pepe's shoulders. Gruffly, he said, "Will get this beat old man, don't you worry."

Then Alastair released Pepe and threw his arms around Cameron. "The great Dragon Chef of New York."

Cameron met the Brit solidly, eye to eye, "Al, good to see you, I didn't expect you to meet us in Nairobi." Cameron flashed a glance at Pepe, then back to Alastair, "I'm sorry it's under these circumstances."

"Me too," said Alastair. "That's why I came myself. I don't want you to have to waste time." He grabbed the shoulder of the dark haired man to his side. "This gentleman is Ari. The best bush pilot I know, and Ari, this is Kincaid and Pepe. My brothers."

Pepe and Cameron in turn each shook Ari's hand.

"Ari will be taking us out to Lanta. First we will need to get you checked in," said Alastair. He spun around to search back toward the terminal, scanning the tarmac until he found what they needed. Near the hatch of a small plane, two Kenyans in customs uniforms were reviewing a clipboard. Alastair raised his hand to signal. One of the uniformed men responded with a nod.

"Do you have any other bags?" asked Alastair.

"This is it," said Cameron, referring to the duffels he and Pepe each held on their shoulders.

"Good," said Alastair. "That way we don't need to go inside."

The uniformed man approached the four men.

"Get your papers ready," said Alastair. "I assume you're travelling French."

"Whenever I can help it," said Pepe.

"Ha, that's funny. I'll take them please."

Alastair lifted his arm in the direction of Cameron and Pepe as the customs agent approached. "These are the two men I told you about." With his other arm, Alastair presented their passports. The man's face held little expression. The agent slowed as he neared, a self-righteous scowl crawled across his face, and then he stepped closely in front of Alastair to receive the passports. Alastair may have paid this man, yet the sudden drop of his brow and quick pierce of his eyes removed any ambiguity, he was charged a fee for service, not for employ. The agent flashed a quick glance at the other three men beside Alastair to ensure all eyes were on him, for what good is power without witness. Without opening either passport, the agent unsnapped a leather pouch on his belt, dug his fingers around inside, and then took out an automatic rubber stamp. He flipped open the first passport to the last page with no interest in seeing the photo. The uniformed man placed the automated stamp on the page and then peered up at the four men under the rim of his hat, his eyes scanning in a threat of authority.

"No other bags?"

Alastair answered quickly, "No."

The customs agent pushed down on the stamp, flipped the other passport open, and brought the stamp down again in one smooth action. He handed the passports back, then slipped the stamp back into his pouch.

The customs man pulled slightly at the front of his hat, "Good evening, gentlemen." The men nodded in return as the uniformed man headed back toward his colleague.

"That was efficient," said Cameron.

Alastair sighed, "Cheap as well. Pretentious lot, these airport trolls."

"My helicopter is over here," said Ari.

"Let's get to it before somebody we don't know starts asking questions," said Alastair.

They walked toward the small planes near the domestic end of the terminal. That end of the terminal was dark; there were not that many flights that came through Nairobi at night. The area of tarmac past the planes was also without light. With the terminal and runway lights to their backs, they could only see a short way in front of them, after that, only darkness.

The night enveloped them and then the stars revealed themselves.

Cameron could not resist looking into the early evening equatorial sky. Few, if any, stars could be seen from Manhattan. Above and around him was the Milky Way, seemingly close enough to touch. He sought out the distant horizon and then let his eyes circle above, around, and back to the terminal, an oasis behind them, a luminous dome that had shielded the stars from them moments before, now silhouetted with a million points of light.

In front of them, the dark form of the helicopter further materialized with each step.

Ari opened the side and then front doors. "Al, you'll want to get your mates set," said Ari, and then he climbed up into the cockpit.

Pepe leaned over to Alastair, "Do you usually fly at

night?"

"Heh, heh, no worries," said Alastair softly, "Most don't. Ari can, by instruments or blindfolded." He clutched the bridge of his nose between his thumb and middle finger, pressing his index finger into his forehead. "Like a pigeon."

A light flipped on inside the cabin. Alastair grabbed an interior handle to pull himself up. Pepe grabbed his arm, stopping him.

"I don't want him to fly blindfolded," said Pepe.

"He won't have to," said Alastair. "Ari learned to fly in the Israeli military, he can comb the bush and desert better than most anyone." Alastair turned his head to Cameron, then back to Pepe, "Then there is the intelligence training."

"Ari is Mossad?" asked Cameron.

"Was, is, does it matter?"

"Not at all," said Pepe. He let loose Alastair's arm.

Alastair flashed his eyes at Cameron.

"It's never mattered to me," said Cameron.

Alastair grinned and then pulled himself up. Alastair opened a panel and then Cameron and Pepe in turn tossed him their duffels to stow. After he secured the panel, he climbed back out of the chopper, circled around to the other side of the cockpit, and then jumped up front. Ari was finishing his preflight checklist. Pepe and Cameron boarded the cabin and fastened their seat belts. Panels separated Alastair and Ari from the rear cabin. Between the panels was an opening. Alastair leaned into the opening and handed back two aviator headsets.

"I brought the good ones, you can jack them up above," said Alastair.

Cameron took the headsets and handed a one to Pepe. Across the side of the large clunky headphones was the word Bose. The headsets were heavily cushioned on the top and around the large earpieces. Cameron slipped the velvet pillow equivalent over his head. When he jacked them, the air sucked away from his inner ears. Cameron pressed a hand up on each earpiece, opened his mouth wide, and moved his jaw around to see if his ears would pop. To his side Cameron could see that Pepe was doing the same. While his jaw was twitching side to side, he glanced up toward the front of the cabin to see Alastair smiling back. Alastair tapped a small switch on his headset and then tapped his earpiece.

"These A20's have noise cancelation," said Alastair.

Cameron could hear him through the headset crystal clear.

"Christ, these are great," Alastair continued, a sudden serious look across his face. "These would have been so nice when we were lads coming up."

Pepe said something that sounded muffled. Alastair placed his finger near the switch on his headphones and Pepe found his. Pepe spoke again, this time Cameron could hear him clearly as well.

"These are nice," said Pepe. "I need a pair of these."

"No problem, mate. I'll put a pair in the post for Christmas."

"This is style," said Pepe.

"The best of the best," said Ari through the headsets. "This is a Eurocopter AS 350 B3plus Squirrel, also known as the Dark Star. This little baby can go anywhere from the bush to the top of Everest."

Pepe pushed his lower lip high, "You mean somebody landed one of these on top of Everest?"

"Heh," said Ari. "I mean I landed one of these on top of Everest."

Cameron and Pepe watched Ari flip a switch above the windscreen and then heard his voice again.

"Dark Star 1 requests engine start, Mount Kenya, Flight Level 320, two passengers, two crew, eleven and a half hours of fuel."

A voice from the tower came over the headsets, "Clearance to Mount Kenya, Dark Star 1."

CHAPTER 9
LAIKIPIA PLATEAU

Pepe was finally able to sleep. Countless ops in years past spent in the backs of planes, trucks, and boats made the copter, gliding softly through the hot Kenyan night, as comfortable as a waterbed. The light ache of fatigue in Cameron's thighs and feet reminded him how they had spent the last twenty hours. Cameron had slept as they crossed the Atlantic. Pepe had never closed his eyes.

The dense blanket of lights that had been Nairobi had funneled out into streams of wide lit super highways that in turn diminished to single lane roads, and then eventually stray beacons in the landscape. The course of the copter was a direct flight path. The silhouette of the far off mountains remained constant against the African sky and Ari maintained a bead toward the highest point in the horizon.

"Take a look to your left," said Alastair.

Cameron leaned forward and peered down at the ground. Below them, among a field of black, was a large thick glowing white crescent.

"Beautiful," said Cameron. "Is that a hydroelectric dam?"

"No, not yet anyway," said Alastair. "They call that the Fourteen Falls. The eight lane highway out of Nairobi may reach here soon."

"Really," said Cameron.

"Bloody shame," said Alastair. "We're on a bit further on. Relax if you can."

Soothed by the subtle vibrations, Cameron rested his head against the wall of the copter and closed his eyes.

~*~

Christine shifted her weight to her side and threw a hand onto each of Cameron's shoulders, pinning him on the picnic blanket. The loose strands of her mussed chestnut hair glowed from the sunlight above, creating a halo around her smiling face.

"Hey," said Cameron.

"Why can't you just tell me when you are going back to the island," said Christine.

"Why so many questions?" asked Cameron. Before Christine could say another word, he reached up and pulled her next to him on the blanket, so that they faced each other side by side. Christine lifted her brow, sighed, and rolled onto her back.

"So that is it. You are the man of mystery," said Christine.

Cameron remained on his side facing Christine. He softly drew his finger down the bridge of Christine's nose, then onto her lips. She lightly kissed his finger, then staring up through the branches of the oak, took his hand into hers.

"I like that you're man of mystery," said Cameron.

"Does it please you to taunt me?"

"Taunt you? How so?"

"You tease me by not telling me when you and Pepe have to return to base. You make me anxious," said Christine.

Cameron rolled from his side onto his back so that

they were both now gazing up into the branches of the oak tree.

"I thought there would be less pressure if you did not have to count down the minutes until I left again. I thought that if we could enjoy all of our time together, our time would not diminish."

"Men," said Christine.

"What does that mean?"

"You think of yourself always. You know when you are going to leave. By doing this you do not spare me anxiety. You make me anxious."

"I make you anxious?"

"You upset me because I do not foolishly think we have all of time. I feel you could leave at any time. I feel you are always going to leave."

~*~

Cameron awoke to the jarring of the copter touching down. Ari switched off the rotors and began to power down the engine. Beyond the windscreen, the shrub filled flat landscape to the east rolled far out to a predawn eastern horizon, lit with hues of fuchsia and vanilla. Through the side window, night still held. Through the thin tree line, Cameron could make out a structure in the dim light, not far from the copter.

"Here we are," said Alastair. "Lanta Resort in the heart of the Laikipia wild country."

"Wild country?" asked Pepe.

"Well, Lanta is a bit of an oasis as are a few other resorts about the area. We are, however, in the central highlands of Kenya. Laikipia covers almost two million acres from the Rift Valley in the west to Mount Kenya in the East. The main lodge is over the ridge. You will be bunking with us in the cottage."

Alastair glanced to the back of the cabin to inspect Cameron and Pepe and then pulled the jack of his headset out of the console to stow. Cameron and Pepe did the same and the three exited the copter leaving Ari to finish his post flight duties.

Alastair led Cameron and Pepe to a slate path that slightly inclined toward the cottage, a fairly modern building, new perhaps forty years prior, built on a small ridge. The light was coming on fast, and though they could not see far into the surrounding morning, the ground and grass at their feet and the trees nearest them were detailed and clear. At the top of the path were wooden steps that led up to a deck. Pepe and Cameron trudged behind Alastair across the deck and then waited for him to unlock the glass door.

"Pepe, will you look at that," said Cameron, looking back at the copter. Their climb had been short and gradual. The deck was above the tops of the small acacia trees, elevated enough to exaggerate their vista of the horizon.

"Hmm," said Pepe.

Having unlocked the door, Alastair now joined them. "She's a beauty. The sunrise is close to breaking. Wait 'til then."

Pepe turned toward the door, placed his hand on Alastair's shoulder, and then walked past. "I'd rather not wait."

Cameron and Alastair peered at each other. Ari stepped onto the deck. "Is he okay?"

"Not yet," said Cameron. "He will be, when his sister is safe."

CHAPTER 10
LAIKIPIA PLATEAU

Behind the billiards table, a large map of Kenya and the Northeast African Coast filled the wall. Crackled decoupage and hues of patina gave the map, no more than a few years old, an antiqued quality that dominated the decor of the game room. Tribal knick-knacks carved as tourist souvenirs were scattered across shelves along with a myriad of classic novels.

"While you were sleeping, I checked the service Pepe set up," said Alastair. "Your friend in London not only left a name for us, he also told us the location of the Kalinihta."

"My sister," said Pepe.

"Yes, your sister, and the crew."

Alastair put his finger in the center of the area of the map marked Kenya. "We are here, and he said," he dragged his finger across the wall to the southern Somali coastline, "the Kalinihta was brought to port here. A bit south of where we would expect. We knew the GPS coordinates from Langdon, of course. Now we have specifics."

"I am guessing that intel came quickly," said Cameron.

"You most likely had not even left the Heathrow tarmac. How did you know?" asked Alastair.

"The man in London was General Ibrahim Dada," said Pepe. "We recognized him straight away."

"Ibrahim Dada?" asked Ari. "He goes by Admiral Dada now. If there were a pirate king, he would be the man. What is he doing in London?"

"Admiral, eh?" said Cameron. "Well, he told us he was a diplomat. I don't think he realized we knew who he was."

"I have heard this before," said Ari, "high-level pirates working with the Somali Government to cut out the low-level competition. How did you recognize him?"

"A past life," said Alastair. "The boys and I met up with Dada's lot outside Mogadishu when we were active. He was a warlord calling himself General Dada then. He became Fleet Admiral when he took over the Somali Marines."

"The Somali Marines?" asked Cameron.

"Marines as in fishermen," said Alastair. "At least that is how they started out. While Dada and his cronies were battling it out inland, Russian and Chinese trawlers moved into Somali waters. You know the story. At first, the fishermen just banded together to defend their fishing waters, cutting off the trawlers with their speedboats. Soon they were organized into four main groups," Alastair pointed to different areas of the coast, "the National Volunteer Coast Guard here in the south, the Merca Group above them, here below Mogadishu, the Somali Marines based out of Haradera ran the coast north of Mogadishu, all along here, and the Puntland Group close to the horn here. The big fisheries caught on to pay to fish, and wasn't too long before the fishermen had a new lucrative business."

"Why sell your fish at market when you can sell them at sea," said Cameron.

"Exactly," said Ari. "That is when Dada took notice."

Alastair continued, "Dada took over the Somali Marines and expanded business. Under his leadership, they evolved to be the most powerful and sophisticated of the pirate groups with a military structure, an admiral, vice-admiral, a head of financial operations, and of course, Dada appointed himself as fleet admiral. Hell, he has a bloody navy to go with his army."

"Yesterday's warlord is today's pirate," said Cameron.

"Today's diplomat," Pepe corrected.

"I suppose," said Cameron. "And the people of Somali?"

Alastair frowned, "Those that have not been recruited by Al Shabaab are at the mercy of the warlords, as always. Starving, desperate, a lot of the crimes that actually go reported are the desperate poor or rogue soldiers not following orders."

"Or street thugs," said Ari.

"Well, once they take up the sword," said Alastair, "they're all thugs in the end."

"I don't know about that," said Cameron. "Anyway, Alastair, you said the Kalinihta was a bit south of where you would expect. We had the coordinates, why would you say that?"

"I meant for a hijacking. These pirates essentially operate as cartels with established territories. The Kalinihta first headed toward Mogadishu, then south. I thought the port a bit of an odd choice. Well, that was before I knew that the message came from Dada. Now it makes perfect sense. As Ari said, high-level pirates like Dada have been working with the Somali Government to cut out the low-level competition. So far the Merca Group has been pretty much forced out and Dada's people have moved in," Alastair drew his finger down the coast, "Dada's message said Abbo Mohammed of the National Volunteer Coast Guard took the Kalinihta." His finger stopped on a port town south of the location of the Kalinihta. "Their territory is pretty specific to Kismayu," he then dragged his finger back up to the reported coordinates. "The yacht came to port in a territory that belonged to the Merca Group and is now predominately run by the Somali Marines."

"That explains how Dada knew so quickly. The Coast

Guard are expanding their operations northward into his new territory," said Cameron.

"And he does not like it," said Alastair.

"That also explains why the men in the garage wanted us to stay away," said Pepe. "I am sure Dada was more than happy to pass along this information."

"Hell, we're doing him a favor," said Ari. "That's absolutely beautiful."

"Strange bedfellows, surely gentlemen, regardless of where they are spreading out landside, the attack in the Seychelles is consistent with the International Maritime Organization records," said Alastair. "The Coast Guard have been seen out that way recently so this is only more reason to believe that we will find the Kalinihta there." Alastair saw Pepe's brow drop and added, "and that is where we will save Christine."

"Great," said Cameron. "Let's get to it."

"Right," said Alastair. "Listen, I have a confession. I didn't want to mention this until the two of you had rested."

"Mention what?" asked Cameron.

An array of framed photographs covered the sidewall of the game room. Portraits and vistas featuring Alastair posing with resort guests, many recognizable celebrities, at various locations around Laikipia. "You see that photo, second from the left," said Alastair. "The one with the elephant cub."

Pepe pointed toward one of the photos, "Here?"

"No," Alastair approached the wall. "This one," he gestured at a photo of himself and another man kneeling on either side of an elephant cub.

"Yes, so?" said Pepe.

"That is a picture of my friend, Nikos Stratos," said Alastair.

"You know Nikos?" asked Pepe.

"Well enough. He has stayed at the resort more than once."

"So you know him," said Pepe.

"I know him, and his father Demetrius."

"And you called his father?" said Cameron.

"And I called his father."

"And?" asked Pepe. "Has the Kalinihta been reported missing?"

"No. The yacht still has not been reported missing, though Demetrius did not seem surprised to hear she was. He has given us substantial funding. Nikos' father would like to see everyone safe. As he puts it, he is greatly disturbed by the circumstances, yet finds relief in that we are able to assist."

"Sounds a bit cold," said Cameron.

"He is Greek, I assure you he is not cold. Cunning yes, not cold."

"The Kalinihta still has not been reported missing," said Pepe. "Langdon's people would have contacted him as well."

"You do not get to where Demetrius Stratos is without holding a few cards. To report the Kalinihta would be to tell the world that he, a shipping magnate, could not even be trusted to care for his own personal craft. I am sure he already had a team assembled before I called. We are a convenience."

"True enough," said Cameron. "Do we have a place to put this funding to use?"

Pepe smiled, "I already know the answer to this."

"You mind sharing?"

"Some ballistics boys," said Pepe.

"A couple of Ari's mates," said Alastair. "You'll like these guys. He leaned his shoulder against the wall and glanced down at the floor, lowering his voice, "They're blooming crazy."

Cameron winked at Alastair. "Great, and when do we head out to see these fellas?"

"We are to meet with them tonight, after dark," said Alastair. "So I had cook prepare a meal. I think we grab a bite now, put our heads down for a kip until dusk, then head to their bunker. They already know the target and have started the logistics." Alastair then peered at Pepe. "Brother, we'll have your sister safe at sun up."

Pepe raised his brow and conjured a smile.

"Did you say bunker?" asked Cameron.

"Heh, yes," said Ari. "That is why we leave at dusk. They don't take well to daytime visitors."

CHAPTER 11
LAIKIPIA PLATEAU

An array of dishes had been prepared in the main house and then brought to the large table on the cottage veranda. Bowls of fresh fruits and platters of vegetables orbited a large centerpiece tray that held a mixed grill of lamb, beef, and chicken smothered in long green beans.

Though there were only four men eating, there was enough food for eight.

Alastair grinned at Cameron and then said, "I think you will find the cuisine sufficient."

"This spread is a feast," said Cameron.

"Well, cook does a fine job regardless. Yet when he heard he was preparing for the Dragon Chef, he may have gone a bit overboard."

"You told him the Dragon Chef was coming?" asked Cameron.

Alastair stared deeply into Cameron's eyes and held his face straight until Pepe, for the first time since arriving from New York, became his usual jovial self with a blurt of laughter.

"Are you daft?" asked Alastair. "If I told him such a thing the entire staff would be running for the hills."

Ari took a seat at the table, "They would have been expecting a giant Komodo lizard man, I would imagine."

Cameron slightly frowned and let his cheeks pucker as he sat, "What is this in these little glass jars?"

Beside each plate was a small jar filled with a mix of what appeared to be diced apples and vegetables.

"That is a house specialty, spiced courgette chutney," said Alastair.

"Really? Courgettes?" asked Cameron.

"Courgettes, tomatoes, onions, garlic, and ginger with a mix of brown sugar and spices. I figured this would get your attention."

"This is good," said Pepe, already sampling a jar.

Ari offered to pour the wine. "I think you will find the wine to your liking as well," he said. He filled the glasses in front of the four, all now seated. "The vines grow not far from here. Though you probably do not want too much for now."

Pepe raised his brow, "Well, we do not want too little."

"I'll drink to that," said Alastair. "Cheers."

"Cheers," the other three echoed as they touched their glasses together.

The toast was more than a mere token. Though Cameron had just met Ari, he knew he was kin to him. They were all kin, the four men at the table. They were brothers-in-arms, veterans of the hidden and silent shadow wars that were the true commerce of government.

Ari had his training in the Israeli forces, then later Mossad. The other three men were at one time Legionnaire super commandos, and later served clandestine as well. Cameron was not alone in Corsica, home of the Second Foreign Parachute Regiment. Alastair and Pepe were members of the special elite unit as well, the elite of the elite. The training that almost killed Cameron, had exacted the same toll on the other two, and the three were among the few to land a Dragon badge, the badge of a commando. The Green Dragons at this table were part of the same team; they had gone from being the tip of the fighting spear on the battlefield to global undercover operations, from the cites of the new fallen eastern bloc to the newly democratized Mongolia.

A little wine was good.

Regardless of their native born nationalities, being in the French Foreign Legion meant they could easily pass the hours with drink. For a brief time, Pepe was smiling, eating, and drinking, and as the tangerine bush of Laikipia, extending from the veranda out to the horizon, began to give way to darker hues of rust, and the cotton white clouds creamed to vanilla, then gold, Cameron could almost forget why they had traveled to Kenya. They could be in Laikipia merely to see their old brother-in-arms once again. Yet as the evening waned, Cameron could see that if a pause lagged too long between a story or a joke, the corners of Pepe's face would begin to drop. They would not be going in anytime soon to earn the rest they needed for the mission to come, rather they would fortify their friend. Each time there was a gap, Cameron was alert to fill the space. That is, if Alastair, also sensitive to the pain behind Pepe's veil, did not fill the void first.

Alastair was the one to finally lure them from the table, before a fall of silence could imminently take hold. Terry, a tall Maasai in the shirtless garb of the local Laikipiak people, came onto the veranda to clear the last of the platters. Only Alastair took note of Terry's soft glance away from the table.

"What is it, Terry?" asked Alastair.

In a nonchalant manner, Terry answered, "She's back."

Alastair stood from his chair and then peered hard out past the acacia trees at the far end of the cottage.

"Oh, you fellas will love this," said Alastair. From inside the French doors he grabbed a pair of binoculars from the side table, and then headed to the edge of the deck. The other three remained in their seats.

"Well, c'mon then," said Alastair to the other three,

already scanning the acacias with his binoculars.

Cameron and Pepe joined Alastair by his side. Ari stayed behind them. Alastair fixed the binoculars on a point past the last tree, then handed the glasses to Pepe.

"What do ya think?" asked Alastair.

"She's beautiful," said Pepe, and then shared the binoculars with Cameron.

Lurking slowly through the brush beneath the tree was a leopard.

"What is she doing out this early?" asked Cameron.

"She is moving closer to where she will want to hunt tonight. Now she will rest," said Alastair.

"We should do the same," said Pepe. "In a short time we must go."

CHAPTER 12
LAIKIPIA PLATEAU

Alastair leaned forward to scan the inky darkness.

"We're close now," said Alastair.

"And there it is," said Ari.

To the southwest of their position, Cameron saw the spent phosphorus cartridge of a flare-gun arc up and then burst high in the air. Ari piloted the helicopter toward where the flare had ignited. As they approached, first one, two, then three bright green fluorescent dots appeared below, forming a triangle. Ari landed the helicopter in the middle of the makeshift landing zone.

"I'm going to power down to save fuel," said Ari, flipping a series of switches that cut power to the rotors.

"Most pilots like hot action," said Cameron. "To keep the equipment running for efficiency."

"I told you," said Ari, "This is an AS 350. This little squirrel will start cold every time."

The last few interior lights flicked off and the cabin flooded with the green glow of the fluorescent signal sticks that surrounded the helicopter. Cameron unplugged the headset from the jack above and slipped the Bose from his head. He opened his mouth and worked his jaw side to side to ease the pressure on his ears.

"Let's hit it," said Alastair, disappearing from his seat into the night. Abruptly, he stuck his head back into the copter. "Oh, careful of the wait-a-bit trees."

"Wait-a-bit trees?" asked Pepe.

"Acacia with thorns like cats claws. They grab you then you have to wait-a-bit to get free."

"Ah."

Alastair pulled his head back into the night.

The other three men exited the copter, the darkness surrounding the makeshift-landing zone chirping to an incessant beat.

"All alone in the wild," said Pepe.

"I assure you, we're far from alone," said Alastair. "If you had your infrared specs on you would see we're standing in the middle of a crowd."

On cue, a hyena cackled in the night. Then, in front of the copter, at the edge of the landing zone, a flashlight switched on. Alastair held his hand up over his eyes.

"Christ, mate, watch it with the torch."

The beam lowered.

"Sorry about that," a deep voice said from behind the light. "This way." The accent was Dutch. The man was Afrikaner.

"Just a minute, boys," said Alastair. He and Ari each switched on their own flashlights. "Here's a torch for each of you," said Alastair. Under his beam, he held two mini Maglites.

Cameron and Pepe took the Maglites, twisted them on, then all four men walked toward the deep voiced man.

Cameron had initially thought the man was holding his light at his shoulder. Then Cameron stepped behind the giant and briefly shined his beam the length of the man. In the dark, Cameron could not gauge the true height of the man.

Pepe whispered into Cameron's ear, "Two meters, and maybe five centimeters."

"Close," said the deep voice. "Two meters, ten centimeters."

"That's Dakarai," said Alastair. "We call him Charlie."

"Pleased to meet you," said Dakarai, without turning back.

"And you," said Pepe.

Away from the green fluorescence, their eyes adjusted quickly. The beam of Dakarai's light ahead, cut with his tree high silhouette, rendered their beams unnecessary. The chatter of the wild heightened and lowered as they made their way through the black. A bright celestial blanket, pulled taut to the horizons, surrounded them. The distant mountains tore into the stars and every few steps, branches of the wait-a-bits rose from the brush, cutting into the night sky.

Ten minutes from where Ari had landed the helicopter, the group entered a flattened circle of gravel that somewhat glowed against the night. Even in the darkness, the area appeared to be a landscaped oasis in the middle of the bush, clear with the exception of two small dark structures on opposing sides of the clearing, silent sentinels, not quite the size of proper toolsheds, each barely larger than a phone booth. Dakarai led them to the dark pillar to their right. The terrain of the gravel crunched differently than the sandy red soil they had been hiking through. Not until Dakarai cracked the door did Cameron first hear the tinny resonation of electric guitar riffs. The sound came from a bowel too deep for so small of a structure. The weathered wooden door opened to a small room that revealed the lemon lit outline of a second door. Cameron thought of the TARDIS, a machine that carried Doctor Who, the television time lord, through time and space, a machine that looked like a small phone booth on the outside yet was paradoxically larger within.

Cameron realized where they were going and it was confirmed when Dakarai opened the second door to reveal a shielded room no larger than a broom closet. Illuminating the space was a clear glass bulb dangling from the top of the closet at the end of a rugged insulated wire. The dim filament burned lemon yellow. The wire was staple tacked to the back wall, leading down to another bulb, and then another below the floor where they stood, deep into the ground.

Dakarai took hold of the rungs of a metal ladder fastened to the left sidewall of the closet, then swung inside. "Close the doors on the way down," he said as he glanced down at his feet and then dropped out of sight.

"Really?" said Pepe.

"You are going to love this," said Alastair. "Go ahead."

"You're going to love this," said Pepe, his face scrunched. "You use that phrase too often, I think." Then in a lower voice, "Qui est telle connerie."

Pepe took hold of the rung and leaned over the shaft. He saw Dakarai still sliding several meters below. Pepe lifted his head, "Oh."

"Do it," urged Alastair.

Cameron slapped Pepe on the back, "You weigh enough, you'll drop fast."

"So funny, you two. See you in a moment," said Pepe, and then he too swung himself onto the ladder rung and let himself disappear into the depths below.

Cameron and the others followed Pepe down the shaft that led to a large music-filled tunnel space meters below the surface. More of the insulated wire was strung in a wide mesh across the naked rock ceiling and walls of the tunnel. Rows of tables, workstations setup at many of them, filled the center of the cave. On the far side of the space, next to a freight lift that led up to the other structure in the clearing above, were uniformly stacked pallets of crates.

The music was coming from a console system to their right, set up in a small makeshift entertainment enclave that included leather chairs, a sofa, and a large flat panel that was silently screening a zombie movie. Funnily enough, the images on the screen were aligned with the rough electric guitar blaring out of the oddly out of place tall pyramid speakers. To their left was a kitchenette with a microwave, mini-fridge, portable range, and espresso machine. The back of the tunnel narrowed to a passage that led further into the earth.

At one of the tables, a man with thick magnifier goggles was hunched under an engineer desk lamp, the variety with several joints and springs for precise managed maneuverability. The goggled man was working meticulously on a clamped electronic device. Another man in a safari vest was hovering closely above the first, inspecting the work. Dakarai was at the kitchenette pouring water from a bottle fountain. An air bubble traveled up through the bottle producing a loud glug. The hovering man raised his head toward Dakarai, still almost cheek to cheek with the man working beside him.

"Oh, good. You're back," the man in the safari vest barked, a breath from the ear of the other.

"Really," exclaimed the goggled man, and he jabbed his elbows up to his sides.

"Sorry," scowled Safari as he eased back from the table. He then turned his attention to the group at the entrance, "You made it from the States. You must be exhausted. How about a little pick up, eh? Arabica, grown local." Safari gestured to the espresso machine then began to move toward the kitchenette.

"Cameron, Pepe," said Alastair, "this is Isaac and at the table is Ezekiel."

"Pleasure," said Isaac, "and he likes to be called 'Eazy'. Being so relaxed and all."

Eazy again raised his hands from his work, this time to acknowledge the group. Without removing his magnified goggles he spoke, "Hello, sorry. The pleasure is mine Pepe and... uh."

"Cameron," said Cameron, "a pleasure,"

"I'm sure," said Eazy, already back to his work.

"Excuse him. He went ahead and armed that thing and now the timer is not functioning the way he wants," said Isaac.

"That device is armed?" asked Pepe. He craned his neck to see if he could identify what Eazy was working on.

"I told him the thing was not ready and he still went ahead and armed it."

"I unarmed it," said Eazy, intently focused on the small screwdriver and pliers in his hand.

Isaac raised his voice, "I was standing right next to you. You did not unarm it."

"There, the timer is fixed, and I did too unarm it. See right here," said Eazy, and then he paused and leaned in, "You are right. The thing is armed."

"I told you. I was standing next to you."

"Yes, here we go. I forgot I had to rearm the device in order to disengage and then reengage the timer. All better now."

Cameron and Pepe shared an intent glance with Alastair and then shifted their concerned gaze to Isaac. Isaac looked back blankly.

"You know we are messing with you," said Isaac. He, Eazy, Alastair, and Dakarai all began to laugh, Ari merely grinned.

Cameron and Pepe collectively sighed.

Cameron glanced at Alastair. "They do this often?"

"Any chance they get," said Alastair. "Isaac and Easy are also former Mossad. Their expertise is demolition."

"I get that," said Pepe. "They have what we need?"

"We will hook you up," said Eazy.

"We are more than happy to do so," said Isaac.

"I would love to have some of that coffee you offered," said Cameron.

"Me as well," said Pepe. "Though now I am feeling quite awake."

CHAPTER 13
LAIKIPIA PLATEAU

The group had moved into a large canvas tent in another section of the tunnel. The tent created a sense that they could be anywhere other than below the earth in the abandoned mine turned bunker. They sat along one side of a table that held current weather charts and a paper model of a seaside compound. Before them, a large physical map of the Somali and Kenyan coast hung on the wall, draped with a plastic overlay. The southern Somali coast was heavily marked with coordinates, circles, and crosses in red and black colored pen. The Indian Ocean portion of the map along the right side was plated with several satellite images of the target area terrain and close-ups of the buildings from the compound modeled on the table. On the left side of the map were photographs of the Kalinihta, her crew, Nikos, and Christine.

Cameron recognized the photo of Christine. The image was from a magazine advertisement she had appeared in a few years before for Estée Lauder. Her face had been cropped and enlarged to fill the photo. There were eight pairs of eyes on the wall next to Christine's yet Cameron was drawn to her's alone.

"They call this the Tactical Center," said Alastair.

"I can see why," said Cameron.

Isaac raised himself from the table and approached the map. "I have to tell you that when Alastair rang us, we were happy to jump on board even before we knew the meat of the situation. We want to see those pirates—and this is, of course, whom we are talking about—gone in general." Isaac placed his hands on his hips and peered directly at the map of the Somali coast, studying something that the others in the room could not see. "There have been far too many rumors that Israel is funding the pirates, rumors that say Israel is attempting to secure a presence in the Gulf of Aden." Isaac's voice softened, "Ridiculous, the CIA knows a lot of the ransom money has changed hands in Lebanon."

"We're not here for the politics," said Cameron, his voice elevated.

"Fair enough," said Isaac, and he spun back toward the table. "Let us tell you how we can help you. As I was saying, we were happy to jump on board right away. As you are aware, the Kalinihta," Isaac gestured to the photograph of the yacht, "is owned by billionaire Demetrius Stratos and as Alastair told you, he has already secured substantial funding for our operation."

"Is that how we were able to get the satellite imagery so fast?" asked Cameron.

Eazy spoke up, "There are many international satellites directed at the Middle East region and I have a direct feed into several of them."

Cameron glanced at Alastair and raised his brow. Alastair raised one brow in return. They had utilized satellite imagery like the photographs on the wall on nearly every mission while in the Legion and after, and Cameron was aware that to gain access to the level of detail displayed in these pictures was near impossible. Anyone could pay to task a satellite down to one meter and big money could easily get half of that. These super sharp pictures were down to a quarter of a meter easy.

Eazy anticipated Cameron's next question. "The hacks are old and unnoticeable," he shrugged his shoulders, "maybe tolerated. You know they seldom risk upgrading the firmware. If the upgrade knocks out a satellite, well..." he raised his hands in the air.

"I am glad we have them," said Pepe. "How recent are they?"

"All from within the last twelve hours," said Isaac, "most an hour before sunset, and the infrareds after. We pulled from the birds right after we heard from Alistair. As you can see, the Kalinihta is anchored here as reported." Isaac referenced an aerial picture of the small harbor at the edge of the building compound. The photograph displayed the buildings closest to the water, a small beach, a dock, and man-made break walls hugging around them. At the mouth of the tiny port was a yacht flanked by buoyed skiffs. The detail of the image was pristine. The chaise lounge pillows on the deck of the Kalinihta were clear, as were the side tables.

"The Kalinihta does not take much water. Why not use the dock?" asked Ari.

"Same reason the skiffs don't," said Cameron.

"You're right," said Eazy. "Good eyes."

"We have done this before," said Alastair.

Isaac ran his finger through the center of the picture, "The road is guarded by a tower and from movement we think that building number four, adjacent to the main building number one here on the courtyard, is a barracks. The clearest point of entry is directly through the harbor, up the beach, and right up the steps to the compound." He gestured to an image of the entire complex, "You see here, and by the model on the table. The walls are three meters high surrounding the compound."

"Ah," said Ari, "There is something in the water."

"Mines would be my guess," said Cameron.

"And you would be right. We also have intelligence that the beach is mined," said Isaac. He gestured toward another two photographs, "We have images of individuals crossing so there must be a safe line... Still."

Eazy continued Isaac's thought, "We believe the safe line would be monitored electronically, or at least as guarded. You can see the guards there." He shot the bead of a laser pointer onto three shadows near the water's edge of the compound, two at the ends of the wide steps, and one obvious sentry on the dock.

"Electronically? That's far more high tech than I imagined for these fellas," said Cameron.

"Well, that is the meat of it," said Isaac.

"How's that?" asked Cameron.

"One of the reasons our friend Dada was so glad to help," said Alastair. "This is not only a stronghold of the National Volunteer Coast Guard. According to Dada this is the home of their leader Abbo Mohammed."

"Their leader?" asked Ari.

"And all that implies," said Isaac. "A lot of men, a lot of guns, and I expect an RPG or two."

"The man that wanted us out of the way," said Cameron.

"The bald man in London Alastair was telling us about?" asked Isaac.

Cameron nodded his head, "I think this is pretty straight forward then, we do a helodrop a kilometer out, then take the yacht from the water."

"I thought you would see it that way. Our helicopter is a modified Sikorsky Black Hawk. She's already fueled and loaded in the launch bay."

"In the launch bay? This place is full of surprises," said Cameron.

Isaac nodded at Cameron. "I think you will find we have all of the gear you require in the armory," said Isaac. "We leave in three hours."

"And if they are not all on the boat?" asked Ari.

"Need be, I can clear the way to the compound," said Eazy. "There will be a lot of noise, which means the team going ashore will have to be fast and surgical."

"If anyone has been taken to the main house it will have been my sister," said Pepe. "Cameron and I will go."

"Not without me," said Alastair. He placed a hand upon Pepe's shoulder, "Vive la Légion." Pepe's eyes matched Alastair's, "The Legion is our strength."

CHAPTER 14
SOMALI COAST NORTH OF KISMAYU

Cameron slipped another clip into a pocket of his wetsuit, then for a third time, in the dim light of the cabin, inspected the MP-5 submachine gun he had selected from Isaac and Eazy's armory. The bewildering variety of weapons amassed in their munitions store amused Cameron. A matter of tactical operation protocol was that all of the munitions were interchangeable. Perhaps confidence in experience was high or maybe the years between field and undercover ops had forgiven rigor and set them in their ways, because each armed by personal preference.

In the cockpit were Isaac and Dakarai, the towering Afrikaner. Isaac and Dakarai were to stay on the helo after the drop. Across the cabin of the Black Hawk, Eazy was inspecting his CTAR-21, an Israeli commando submachine gun. Alastair sat next to Eazy with his hands on his lap, his back arrow straight. Pepe was sitting in the back leaning against the corner, inspecting the MP-5 he had selected. Cameron watched Pepe maneuver the safety toggle from single fire to rapid then back to single. Pepe's gaze was not on his weapon. He stared vacuously into the interior of the cabin, sliding the toggle to different hot actions. Cameron recognized that Pepe was running a combat simulation.

Though the small team was well equipped, no one else wanted to see battle this morning. The plan was a direct action infiltration exfiltration, a commando specialization. The four of them were to shadow the yacht with the zodiacs and then rescue the crew. If anyone was missing, Eazy was to evacuate with whatever hostages were on board while the other three went ashore, and they were only going ashore if necessary. Their team was too small to take any great risks. Somewhere outside of the Black Hawk was Ari in the Dark Star. Ari had not hesitated in his role of the mission. If everything went well on the yacht, they would not see Ari again until the mission was complete. If they had to get to the main house on the beach, what they referred to as building number one, then Ari was going to come in like the cavalry, strafing with the guns newly fitted at the bunker, and lift them out, or at least provide cover for the Black Hawk if all of the hostages had been moved to shore.

That was a major kink in the plan.

The team was counting on the hostages being left on the yacht and even with the satellite images that Eazy was able to retrieve, there was no way of knowing if that was the case. The team had debated as to whether the zodiacs should be brought to shore or the Black Hawk brought in. In the end, Pepe made the call. If the compound was still too hot to evacuate with the Black Hack, there was no way the three of them were going the get all of the hostages onto the beach and out. "If we fail, we fail big," said Pepe. So that was Plan A, the yacht, Plan B, the compound with Ari, Plan C, the compound with the Black Hawk, and if Plan C went awry, their last resort Plan D would be the zodiacs on the beach with strafing fire from Ari. No one wanted Plan D. They all agreed the Kalinihta was to be utilized if the yacht had fuel and the captain was in shape to pilot the ship, yet they had no time to discover if the hull was rigged with explosives and they certainly could not outrun the skiffs that would have GPS locks on the yacht.

If the uncertainty bothered any of them, none of them blinked. Cameron, Pepe, and Alastair had been on missions less certain, missions deemed impossible, missions deemed suicide. Cameron did not know the history of his new ex-Mossad and Afrikaner comrades, yet he knew brothers-in-arms. Certainly every soldier regardless of status prefers black and white, but the reality is that every mission is colored with hues of grey. Besides, there was never a time this mission was going to be a no-go. Pepe's sister was being held hostage. Regardless of the financial incentive sent down by Stratos, the three Legionnaires had been destined to make this trip from the moment the Kalinihta was boarded.

Cameron checked if the knives he had strapped on were secure. He unsheathed the knife on his ankle and began to sharpen the blade against a small accompanying stone.

"Look at you," said Pepe.

Cameron lifted his gaze to Pepe, "What?"

"What was that show you were taping? Steel Chef?"

"Uh, ya, something like that," said Cameron.

"Ha, ha, if they could see you now."

"You would probably win more with that steel," said Alastair, his eyes now open. Pepe began to boisterously laugh.

"You could really," said Pepe, having a hard time getting the words out, "put an 'edge' on that show."

Alastair and Eazy now joined in the laughter.

"Might help you 'cut out' the competition," said Alastair, causing the three to laugh even harder.

"Oh, you're funny," said Cameron. "The both of you, clowns." Cameron pointed the end of the blade at Eazy, "What are you laughing for? You even know what they're talking about?"

"I don't need to," said Eazy. "Everyone appreciates the Dragon Chef's 'sharp wit.'"

This caused all three to bellow with laughter.

Cameron raised his brow and shook his head, "Open the door so I can jump out of this bird."

Over their headsets they heard Isaac's voice, "You'll have your wish soon, Dragon. Three minutes to drop. Prep the zodiacs."

The laughter stopped. "Clear," each said into their headsets.

The four men secured their kits and prepped for the door.

Eazy dropped to his knees and pulled two large duffels to the center of the cabin. "We will need one of these in each of the zodiacs."

"Explosives?" asked Pepe.

"More than just that. The contents will get you across the two mine fields if the three of you have to get up to the compound," said Eazy.

Dakarai entered the cabin from the cockpit to open the hatch.

"On target, H2 check in," said Isaac.

"H2 at your eleven," said Ari.

"H2 affirmed," said Isaac. "Open hatch."

Dakarai opened the hatch, "Hatch open," said Dakarai. "Get ready for bump one." Dakarai released the first zodiac and the helo lifted slightly.

Ari's voice came on the headsets, "Zodiac one in the water."

"Get ready for bump two," said Dakarai. He released the second zodiac and the helo lifted again and tilted before straightening out. "She's caught."

Ari's voice came on the radio again, "Zodiac two is dangling."

Dakarai pulled a ten-inch blade from his belt and slipped the edge into his cuff, "Back in two, H1."

"Affirmative," said Isaac. "Don't damage the boat, we only brought two."

Dakarai slipped over the side.

The team did not need to wait long. In less than a

minute, the helo lifted slightly.

"H1, Zodiac two is in the water," said Ari.

Dakarai put an arm up onto the hatch and then Eazy and Pepe pulled him in.

Dakarai composed himself quickly and swung around into position, "You should be able to stay dry. The water is glass, the boats are below."

"Great. Let's drop the ropes," said Pepe.

As soon as the ropes were uncoiled, Pepe and Eazy stepped into their positions to fast rope.

"Team ready, H1," said Dakarai.

"Then team clear," said Isaac.

Eazy and Pepe slid down the ropes into a zodiac below. As soon as they were clear of the ropes, they secured the zodiacs together while on the helo Alastair and Cameron clipped the first duffel onto the ropes.

"Package ready," said Dakarai.

"Ready for package," said Eazy.

Cameron and Alastair let the duffel drop. Eazy and Pepe secured it and then moved the duffel to the second zodiac.

"Package ready."

"Ready for package."

The second duffel dropped from the helo onto the zodiac, followed by Alastair and then Cameron.

"Team clear," said Dakarai.

"Team is in the water," said Ari.

"See you soon, boys," said Isaac.

The two helicopters moved off and within minutes the zodiacs were separated and motoring toward shore.

CHAPTER 15
ABBO'S COMPOUND

The equatorial sky densely glittered above while below the two zodiacs glided across the mirrored surface of the early morning ocean. The water was so still and silent that the two-man crews had pulled the rotors up and were now bent over the sides rowing in rapid uniform pace. Before the small inflatable crafts, the profile of the Kalinihta glowed white bow to stern, hugged between the two hilly shadows of the breakwalls that extended out into the water beside her. On shore, the compound was dark, no lights in the windows, or the exterior, and the western sky beyond the large structure, darkest before the dawn.

Careful to not nudge the hull too harshly, the team gently steered the zodiacs to the stern of the Kalinihta. Pepe eased a small mirror around the corner of the swim platform. He flashed a hand gesture to Cameron and Alastair to signal the deck was clear. The crews used their hands to slide the crafts along the hull and then when the first zodiac was in position, Pepe rolled from the inflatable up onto the platform, keeping out of view of the aft deck and salon steps above. Pepe extended his mirror, then pointed two fingers at his eyes. This meant the salon was dark and that they would need the night vision gear. Eazy quietly handed each of the three men a headset that included a monocular lens and a battery pack. Alastair and Cameron fit their gear into place; Pepe passed, preferring to trust the darkness.

In three quick movements, Cameron allowed himself to be boosted by Alastair up onto the deck and into a gun ready point position. To his left, the Jacuzzi sat flat, reflecting iridescent green to his night glass; on his right, the chaise lounges were unspoiled. Cameron scanned the dark void of the aft salon through the open glass doors. The ceiling mirror and heavy metal trim brought a lot of light into his scope. He took three hunched steps forward, ready to dodge if needed. The luxury of the fine wood paneled lounge was in no less a state than earlier in the week. Original artwork still adorned the walls and the fabrics of the cushions, though tinted green by the night glass, were untainted. The neat and unwrinkled placement of the pillows on the furniture did not appear to be in any way abnormal. The Kalinihta was in stasis, immune to the circumstance of her crew.

Alastair sidled Cameron's left and then Pepe his right.

The three men shared a glance and a nod. They had reviewed blueprints of the Kalinihta at the bunker. There were two decks above, the sky deck and top deck, and below were the cabins and engine room. Alastair was to work his way skyward, Cameron to the bow, and Pepe was going to the compartments below where most likely the hostages—and his sister—were being held. A standard sweep the three had performed countless times before. Eazy was to stay with the zodiacs unless requested.

The three strode forward in unison, a rhythmic machine, Alastair and Cameron with MP-5s ready and Pepe wielding a blade. At the back of the salon, a decorative spiral staircase shot up to the sky deck while to the side a second stairwell slipped to the stateroom and guest cabins below. At the point of the stairwells, Pepe and Alastair split off to their own appropriate preplanned routes. Cameron pressed forward toward the bow of the yacht.

Cameron entered the dining salon next. The large dining table and small side bar were in order, as was the rest of the lounge, preserved as the aft salon had been. Even the compliment of liquor lining the corner-mirrored shelves above the bar was untouched. Then again, the men who took the yacht did not think of themselves as pirates, rather as an Islamic coastguard, and as such were Muslims bound to a Sharia law prohibiting alcohol. The team's overall boarding plan took advantage of the fact that these captors were likely devout. In moments, dawn would begin and the morning call to prayer would come. As worshipers of Islam, the devout believe God's most favored prayer of the day is the Fajr dawn prayer. Muslims believe all others sleep while the devout pray. The plan hinged on infiltrating the yacht, and then, if necessary, the compound, just before the prayer, and then evacuating while surrounding reinforcements were still praying.

A large mural of a silver olive tree covered the wall at the back of the dining salon. Cameron knew from the blueprints that a television was behind a retractable panel and that behind that was the galley. On either side of the wall was a door, the one to the left would lead up to the pilot house, the one to the right would lead down to the crew's mess. Cameron placed his back near the edge of the left side entryway, then eased the door open. The hallway was dimly lit from the forward pilothouse. He disengaged his night glass so as not to be blinded by a flood of light. From a pocket, Cameron pulled a thin scope and then began to ease the glass to the corner to catch the reflection. When he noticed how reflective the dim light was on the gold trim of the hallway sconce, he stopped. The scope could betray him, yet the fixture could be his ally. Cameron slipped the scope back into his sleeve pocket and then nuzzled close to the corner to use the sconce fixture as a mirror. Within the golden shine was a pocket of clarity, a slight window of reflection onto the helm. In the image, Cameron saw a man hunched forward.

Cameron pivoted the edge of the door and swung into the galley with a sense of immediacy.

The galley was empty.

Cameron took in a breath and then burst around the corner of the hallway onto the four-step stairwell leading up to the pilothouse. The MP-5 leading, he steadily marched up the short steps, and when in contact squeezed the trigger twice. The only sound was the rapid clack of the bolt and the clink of the two metal casings hitting the floor, rapidly followed by two more. The second man in the pilothouse, the man that had not been in Cameron's view, did not even have time to turn to see what had caused the sound of the first two clinks. Cameron had not had to think. The decision to shoot the second man was neither rational nor irrational, not a decision at all, not instinct, merely a simple motor response, even after all the years away from active duty. Vive la Légion.

Cameron placed a finger to his headset, "Helm clear."

"Top clear," said Alastair. Cameron crossed the pilothouse to ensure the other entrance was clear, then entered the sky deck. Alastair was already crossing the lounge.

"Any resistance?" asked Cameron.

"Nothing up top except the yacht's tender," said Alastair, "tarped and tethered aft of the communications tower."

The two quickly crossed back through the pilothouse and then slipped back down the steps in the event anyone at the compound or on the breakwall could see into the dimly lit room.

Cameron led Alastair into the cleared galley. They each clipped their night scopes back on. Traversing the galley, Cameron spun quickly toward the crew's mess. There was no light emitting from the stairwell below, yet that did not mean the cabin was empty. Cameron floated down the four steps into the mess, squeezing two rounds into the heads of the men sleeping face down on the table. These devout would not be waking for prayer.

As Cameron made his way back up the short stairwell, Pepe's voice tinned into his ear, "Below deck clear."

Cameron nodded to Alastair standing at the door of the dining room.

"Main and top all clear," said Alastair. "Do you have the targets?"

Cameron and Alastair waited a moment for Pepe's reply, then headed for the stairwell when no reply came. Pepe was rapidly climbing the steps.

"Pepe," said Cameron. "The targets?"

"What's going on in there?" asked Eazy.

Pepe stopped at the top of the stairs, "In the stateroom. All but two."

Pepe began to step past Cameron and Alastair.

"Hey, where are you going?" asked Alastair.

"The compound," said Pepe.

CHAPTER 16
ABBO'S COMPOUND

Cameron did not need the light to see the darkness buried deep in Pepe's eyes.

"Just hold on a minute," said Cameron.

Pepe stopped.

Cameron continued, "Let's get those people out of here and storm the compound properly." He placed his hand on Pepe's shoulder, "Together, as planned."

Alastair placed his hand on Pepe's other shoulder, "Vive la Légion."

Pepe inhaled deeply, "Vive la Légion."

"Sounds like you're going in," said Eazy over the headset. "I need one of you to come out here and give me a hand with this gear. I think you'll like what I brought."

"Sure thing," said Pepe.

"The captain was down below?" asked Cameron.

"Yeah, everyone except... and they look pretty good," said Pepe.

"Great, let me go see if he wants to pilot this boat out of here," said Cameron.

Cameron squeezed Pepe's shoulder tightly, then raised his hand and slapped back down. Then Cameron slid around Pepe down into the stairwell. At the bottom of the stairs, the green tint of the scope was far dimmer by comparison to the light-touched upper decks. The lower landing opened to a hallway that led aft to the main stateroom. Immediately adjacent from the landing was a double pane glass door shielding a large collection of wine. Hatches to small cabins lined one side of the hallway, while on the other side there was only the door to the engine room. Cameron knew that Pepe would have swept the engine room first for signs of sabotage, not that they expected any from these captors, only because training is training.

On the floor at the end of the hall, a throat slit body was curled and gnarled with eyes wide and unaware. The door to the stateroom was open and a dim light flowed out. Cameron removed his scope and peeked in. The cook and the two women were seated on the large bed along with the Seychellois. On the sidewall berth sat the captain and the two Genovese.

"You know you are liberated," said Cameron.

The captain, aged by the days and the dark purple contusion along the side of his face, nodded slowly, "Yes. Thank you."

"Are you Lewis?"

"Yes."

"Can you pilot out of here?"

"Yes." The captain's own answer struck him and his eyes lit, "Oh, yes."

"Good. Come with me," said Cameron. "The rest of you, I'm sorry. Unless the captain needs you, you should probably stay out of sight."

Those on the bed nodded their heads while the two Genovese on the berth turned to their captain. The captain met eyes with his crewmen yet directed his question to Cameron. His authority returned to his tone. "Is the yacht clear?"

"Yes."

"Aberto and Donato, you two make ready the engine room," said the captain.

" Sì," said Aberto, echoed by his brother.

"The rest of you stay here as this man said."

"Okay," said Cameron. "Follow my light. Watch your step here by the door."

Cameron made his way back toward the stairwell. The captain was a step behind him. Cameron noticed the captain did not flinch at the body on the floor, nor did the Italians. Cameron stopped at the engine room hatch so that the brothers could see to enter. Once inside, they switched on the interior cabin light and then Cameron and the captain were on their way.

"Thank you," said the captain. "I'm at a disadvantage, you know my name."

"I'm Kincaid. Don't thank me yet. There's a compound full of enemy combatants fifty meters from your hull."

"I see."

"What shape is she in?" asked Cameron.

"She'll motor fine. That's how we got here," said the Captain.

"And fuel?"

"There's enough fuel to get clear. You're thinking south to Lamu?"

"I am."

"We can get there."

At the top of the stairwell, Alastair was waiting in the dark.

"This is Alastair," said Cameron.

"Captain Lewis," said Alastair, nodding. "Cameron, we good to go?"

"Yeah. One more thing, captain, how fast can you push her?"

"We can hold twenty-five knots easy in this clear water. The diesel will burn though," said the captain.

"Twenty-five should be good," said Cameron. "We

only need to clear here."

"Won't they be sending anything after us?" asked the captain.

"I wouldn't worry about them getting too far from shore," said Pepe as he entered the cabin. "Our man has some truly special toys."

"Good to hear," said Cameron. "All right, Captain, we'll leave you to it. Wait for our signal, then haul out of here."

Cameron and Alastair joined Pepe. Alastair gestured to what Pepe was holding in his hands, "What the hell is that?"

"Eazy calls it a lobster," said Pepe.

"A robot lobster," said Eazy over Pepe's shoulder. Eazy held up two more, one in each hand.

The machines were indeed robots and looked remarkably similar to lobsters. The core bodies were large rectangular blocks lined with coils and servos along the sides where eight long insect like legs shot out. From the front of the block were two very long copper antennae and on the tail end a mechanical lobster tail, fin and all. In place of the claws were two large black oval discs, obviously sensor plates of some type.

"What are you going to do with these?" asked Alastair. "Are they mines?"

"The opposite," said Eazy. "We detected mines in the water and on the beach from the satellite shots. These little fellas are going to seek out the underwater mines between us and the compound and..." Eazy lifted his arms in a makeshift explosion, "Boom."

"Heh heh," chuckled Pepe.

"Are you sure this will work?" asked Cameron.

"Yes, of course," said Eazy. "It's biomimetic, a machine designed to function like a biological system. Works perfectly, like a lobster, swims through the water straight to the mine."

"You've done this before?" asked Cameron.

"I've tested blowing things up. I use them mostly for

underwater surveillance."

"He has a lot of them," said Pepe. "If they move through the water the way they're supposed to, they're bound to hit something."

"Hmm," said Alastair.

"With what Stratos is paying I figure I can get some upgrades," said Eazy.

Cameron took an electronic cephalopod from Eazy to observe the metal monstrosity more closely. "These will clear the beach too?"

"No, I have something a bit more conventional for that," said Eazy. He reached into his pocket and pulled out a .50 caliber dart.

"Is that an antipersonnel venom dart?" asked Cameron.

Eazy nodded. "This one is empty," said Eazy. He twirled the long blunt nosed dart between his fingers, "good thing too, because DETA is deadly. I have some modified mortars. These little babies cut through surf and sand like butter. Whatever does not go boom is then neutralized by the DETA. DETA is a caustic chemical."

"Caustic?" said Pepe.

"I would watch my step," said Eazy.

"Sounds good to me. When can these things go into the water?" asked Cameron.

"Whenever the captain is ready."

CHAPTER 17
ABBO'S COMPOUND

The first mine blew halfway between the shore and the Kalinihta. The undersea lobsters were doing their job. The sea erupted into a high pillar, followed immediately by a cascade of others across the small harbor. Eazy and Alastair did not hesitate to launch the first package containing the venom darts. The blunt missile shot up out of the mortar with a loud thunk, arcing above the beach, and then soundlessly separated to release an uncountable number of shadowless spikes high above the surf. A wall of quick shimmer washed in front of the compound as the darts accelerated down. On the metal daggers' point of impact, a rapid succession of detonations blanketed the beach and surf, lifting sand and water high from the shore. Additional liquid columns sprouted up in the harbor as the deep-water mines began to clear, some in reaction to the darts, others to the robot lobsters.

Eazy and Alastair fired another package to clear the remainder of the beach. Before the second package had even arced, Alastair was in the zodiac with Cameron and Pepe. He dropped a knee forward at the bow beside Cameron as Pepe eased the throttle. The inflatable gently lifted above the dark water's surface and floated forward.

On the bridge of the Kalinihta, Captain Lewis eased the throttle forward and began the journey starboard out to sea.

So far, there was no movement from the compound.

If the scene were to be transcended from the zodiac's strongan duotex, the carbon, the steel, and the flesh of the men, to one large piece of marble, no pose would need to change. In the spray of the surf, the faces of these men were statuesque. These men, stoic in their deed, were operating textbook. Pepe was a master with the throttle. The zodiac pressed on with varying momentum to negotiate the bomb made swells. Cameron and Alastair each were prone against the inflated sides of the assault craft's bow, their weapons set to discharge on impulse. Though all three men still had vision gear, none chose to cover. A medley mist of water and harbor bottom coated brows and cheeks with heavy muddy droplets that ran down, and then spouted from, each chin. Their faces were a contrast to the dripping white foam and shadows from the night's last low indigo hues.

The first light of dawn shot from the eastern sky, illuminating the five-story face of the now docile compound and cratered beach. Two boat lengths from shore, a final water column erupted to the starboard of the zodiac, the last of the mines. Four seconds later, Pepe cut the throttle as the craft slid into the bright effervescent spume at the shoreline. In a fluid motion, Alastair launched from the bow, towline in hand, and as he did, two shirtless men with Kalashnikovs ran from a near door. The two men immediately fell, the second falling into the first before either hit the ground. Cameron, positioned to fire again, waited for Pepe to clear the inflatable so they could complete their three-man beachhead.

Cameron, Alastair, and Pepe went directly to the door the two shirtless men had exited from. This shore side structure was main building number one and the most likely to hold hostages. Cameron and Alastair climbed the short porch first. The stucco wall of the compound was caked with muddy sand, as were the steps up the porch to the door. From the side of the building, four men came running out onto the large break wall, oblivious to the three commandos on the beach below them. The four men were yelling and waved behind them to someone unseen and then frantically pointed to the Kalinihta. Cameron raised his MP-5 submachine gun toward the four men and then, before discharging, yielded to Pepe's gesture. Pepe, below the small porch on the beach, could see something Cameron could not and had tilted his MP-5 up on a slight angle. Alastair shifted his attention from the open doorway he and Cameron stood in front of to the side of the compound.

Cameron and Pepe were focused on the four on the breakwall and their unseen friend.

From the edge of the building another man came running to join the first four. On his shoulder, bobbing back and forth as he clumsily jogged, was an RPG-7 already loaded with a single stage warhead. Trailing behind was a younger man, maybe an older boy, half carrying, half dragging three more warheads. The four men on the breakwall were ecstatic, still waving and pointing to the Kalinihta. When the grenadier got into position, Pepe flipped thumbs up to Cameron and in six easy headshots the frantic breakwall mob became a pile of corpses.

The Kalinihta slipped safely south out of view of the small harbor.

Through the outer doorway, a second door, solid iron and locked from the inside, blocked their entrance into the building. Alastair secured a small cake of C4 to each of the two hinges, then signaled Cameron down to the side of the outer doorway. Alastair then slid himself around to the other side of the outer door. Pepe positioned himself on the second step of the porch, hunched clear. With a nod to Cameron and Pepe, Alastair thumb punched the detonator to the explosives. From inside the vestibule came a thud and a mist of dust.

A door opening out was a bad design for security, yet an advantage for the three.

Pepe was the first up and into the vestibule. He immediately assessed the space that once held the upper hinge and from one of his long pockets produced a thick, wide shiv. He jammed the shard into the newly formed crevice. Pepe's portliness gave him easy leverage to jar the heavy metal door to the side.

Alastair and Cameron's MP-5s filled the new-formed void; they found the room empty.

As they had with countless other incursions, Cameron, Pepe and Alastair began to clear the first building of the compound, room by empty room. The rooms were large and interiors out of place for this region and time. The furnishings were fine and intact, paintings, murals, lamps with detailed trim, and the amount of fine woods impeccable. This was truly the refuge of a rich man, and in southern Somalia in these times that meant a warlord.

That each room was coming up empty in the first building did not surprise Cameron. The assault during the Fajr dawn prayer was meant to minimize confrontation.

Still, someone had locked that metal security door behind the first two shirtless men, and somewhere in this building or the next, someone was holding Christine.

CHAPTER 18
ABBO'S COMPOUND

At the beach level, the sheer walls of the compound were windowless in defense of monsoon force or tsunamis that could clear the small harbor breakwalls. The top two stories of the ocean facing building were walled in industrial glass, allowing the dull, blue hued low morning light to wash through. Easily confused with a penthouse suite from any metropolitan city, the upper two floors of the five-story compound were adorned with an array of modern art, luxurious sofas, panel televisions, and flowing white panel curtains that punctuated the ocean vista.

Cameron and Pepe entered the top floor, an open loft space, from a spiral staircase in the center of the room. From where they stood, the room was clear, their only blind spot a short wall behind the stair. The two each chose a different side and circled the divider.

On the other side of the division wall was a lounge. A wooden bar was at the far end and occupying the space between them was an Olympic size billiards table. Seated on the floor at the end of the billiards table was Nikos, his back against the division wall. Nikos was clean, well dressed, and although very shaken and bruised, he appeared otherwise unharmed. Also sitting on the floor, at the end of the billiards table, was a thin man of dark Somali complexion. This second man was also clean and well dressed, yet holding a large golden handgun. He held the gun tightly with both hands wavering to either side of Nikos' head. He held the gun too tightly, as the weapon quivered in his hand.

The gunman did not move his watery glazed eyes away from Nikos. He waved the cannon side to side, his breathing getting noticeably heavier.

Though muffled by the glass and the five floor distance to the courtyard below, yelling could be heard as men rallied to discover what had caused the beach cacophony a few moments before.

Pepe waited and watched the heavy gun, a gold-plated .50 caliber Israeli Desert Eagle, hover in front of Nikos' face. He eyed the man holding the expensive weapon, dressed in a silk shirt, linen slacks, and Prada shoes. Pepe was certain this man had never fired the fancy trophy that he was now waving dangerously in the air. Pepe also knew that the action on the .50 caliber was sensitive and that if this man became any further stressed, there was going to be a hole through Nikos, on through the wall, and into the next building.

Pepe paced the rhythm of the nervous man's breathing with the sway of the .50 caliber, and when the small cannon was pointed at the wall beside Nikos' head, he acted. A shell from the MP-5 made a small clink against the floor and blood from the man's head sprayed Nikos.

"Bloody hell!" said Nikos, his eyes wide, his feet shuffling him into the wall in a failed attempt to put space between himself and the recently departed.

A fleeting moment passed and Nikos sucked in a deep breath, tossing his head back against the wall.

"Êtes-vous d'accord!" said Pepe. "Everything is okay."

Nikos ran his fingers across his face then, seeing blood on the ends, flexed them in an odd attempt to rid them of the stain, "You just blew a hole through Feizel's bloody head."

"Are you okay?" asked Pepe.

"Yes," said Nikos. He began to stand, "I'm fine."

"Where's Christine?" asked Pepe.

"She's gone. They took her," said Nikos. He went to the bar across the billiards table. "By helicopter, two, three days ago."

"Who took her?" asked Cameron. "Did Abbo take her with him?"

"No. Not Abbo. He was never here." Nikos surveyed the bar, then found a bottle of seltzer. "It was the man who boarded the yacht," he doused his hands with the seltzer, "A Somali. A really tall bald fellow."

Cameron flashed his eyes at Pepe, "I think we've met."

The sound of rapid fire and single shots rose up from the courtyard.

"We have multiple shooters out here," said Alastair into the headset. When the shooting had begun, he had gone down to secure the door leading out of the building into the courtyard.

Cameron put his finger to his headset, "Are you engaged?"

"No," said Alastair. "They're shooting at shadows and each other. We better get out of here though. I have a feeling it's going to get pretty hot. You have the packages?"

"We have one package and we are on are way," said Cameron.

Nikos paced to the side of the room, both of his hands clasped behind his head. He spun back to Cameron and Pepe, "This is shit. We're dead. Do you know who you just killed?" Nikos waited for a response that was not coming. Cameron and Pepe watched him with still faces. "Well, do you?" asked Nikos again. "You just blew a hole through the head of Abbo Mohammed's son. We are so dead."

Cameron glanced down at the corpse sprawled below the billiards table, "Is that who that was? Pepe did you know who that was?"

Pepe did not take his eyes away from Nikos, "No."

"Pepe did not know who that was," said Cameron. "I'll tell you this though. If we don't get out of here, you are dead. Your friend Alastair is downstairs if that makes you feel any better."

The presence of someone familiar appeared to calm Nikos, "Alastair is here?"

"For the moment," said Pepe. "Shall we?"

Nikos lowered his hands slowly at first, then dropped them to his sides. "Yes, let's go." Though Nikos was clean, fed, and dressed, his face was horribly bruised. There was no mistake that Nikos had taken a beating.

The three began to walk around the divider. "Wait," said Nikos. He bent over and relieved dead Feizel's still warm hands of the .50 caliber Desert Eagle.

"You sure?" asked Cameron.

Nikos lifted the .50 caliber and pulled the slide back from the barrel, allowing a round to flow into the chamber, "Unlike Feizel, I know how to use this weapon."

CHAPTER 19
ABBO'S COMPOUND

Alastair nodded toward the door that led to the harbor. "We head out onto that beach there is no way to guarantee that inflatable stays inflated." He shifted his gaze to Nikos. Beads of sweat poured from the young Greek. Alastair pursed his lip. "The zodiac is out of the question."

Nikos' tone was rushed, "So that was your plan?"

From the courtyard came a booming concussion, then a barrage of rapid machine gun fire followed by the ever closer rhythmic chopping of rotors.

Alastair stretched the back of his neck, extending his height. "No, that's our plan," Alastair arched a brow, "You remember Ari?"

Nikos bobbed his head, "Of course, right."

Cameron peeked past the edge of the window. The courtyard was full of silhouettes backlit by the stucco of the compound's other buildings, and from above by the indigo glow of the brightening predawn sky. Some shadows were frozen in position while others were frantically trying to evade the sheets of strafing fire from the copter.

"What do we have, Al?" asked Cameron.

"They're consolidated in building four as we

suspected," said Alastair. "The three you see scurrying are positioning from there. From the sounds of it Ari has compromised tower one."

"You left the gifts Eazy packed?"

"I found a beautiful place to stash the satchel."

Cameron nodded and then touched his headset, "H2, check in."

"This is H2," said Ari over the headset. "Are you ready to come home?"

"Affirmative, H2. Four to pick up, repeat, four to pick up. Ready when you are," said Cameron.

"Now is good," said Ari. "Landing zone one, repeat, landing zone one."

The rhythmic chop of the Dark Star rotors grew louder as Ari maneuvered the copter to the clearing they'd designated as landing zone one across the courtyard. The commandos instinctively did a periphery check of their gear, a rapid weapon inspection, and an up down of each other, the type of actions trained into their core.

Cameron placed his hand on the handle of the door. "Nikos, you're going out with Alastair first, then Pepe, you'll go. I'll cover from the back. Straight to the chopper, got it?"

Nikos nodded his head and then Cameron pulled the handle of the door.

Cameron peeked out, his nose filling with the pungent fumes of the burning tower hidden from his view by the barracks. He then threw the door open wide, "Go, go, go!"

Outside warmth flooded into the doorway with the thunderous rotor of the Dark Star copter touching down directly across the courtyard. Nikos and Alastair broke from the building in a dead run. The courtyard was far brighter outside than when Cameron had peered through the window. The silhouettes and shadows now had detail, though nothing showed true color, rather varying hues of blue with the exception of the stucco and stone wall which appeared in odd scales of grey. In a few quick heart pounding seconds, Nikos and Alastair were in the copter.

"Go!" said Cameron.

Pepe launched from the doorway toward the copter.

When Cameron heard the Kalashnikov, he instinctively turned. The rotors muffled the rapid burst, yet the compound walls surrounding the courtyard created a loud echo trail back to the barracks. Fortunately, the shooter had been leading his target too far, so Pepe had seen bullets pummel the top of the stone well at the center of the courtyard in time to dive safely below the line of fire.

Cameron fired at the barrel of the Kalashnikov protruding from the doorway of the barracks. The shooter still had a clear bead on the well and when Pepe tried to ease out of cover, he was chased back with a rapid succession of rounds.

Pepe was pinned down at the well by the shooter.

Cameron expected the inside of the barracks to be wide open and without walls, so he targeted the windows. The barrel in the doorway still did not waver. He decided to go in close and broke into a run toward the side of the barracks. The gunman in the doorway paid no attention to Cameron running along the side of the courtyard. When Cameron reached safety behind the corner, he pulled a grenade from his pocket.

Across the courtyard, Cameron saw another fighter running up behind Pepe's position.

Pepe launched himself from behind the well toward the assailant. One hand to a shoulder and the other to the waist, he hurled the man onto the ground out into the open, away from the well. Like a cat to his feet, the man was back at Pepe fist-to-fist, hand-to-hand. Cameron raised his MP-5. The two men were moving too quickly for Cameron to target and fire.

Alastair's voice shot over the headset, "We have an RPG."

"Where?" asked Cameron.

"The other side of the barracks. Can you get to him,

Kincaid?"

Cameron engaged the grenade he still held and then lobbed the small bomb blindly around the front into the direction of the RPG.

A second later there was an explosion.

Debris shot past the corner where Cameron stood, and a bloody flesh-filled boot landed near his feet. "Did I get him?" asked Cameron.

"No," yelled Alastair over the mic. "The shooter ran out and got in the way. I have a shot. Ari can you lift us up?"

Ari did not hesitate at Alastair's request. The Dark Star lifted to hover above the ground and gently spun to the side. Alastair immediately shot toward the grenadier Cameron could not see. Alastair fired too late or missed, from the far side of the barracks, a rocket flew.

The ghastly slow white smoke trail of the rocket cut across the courtyard, not to the copter as intended, but toward the center of the courtyard. The stone well blew to pieces. Cameron threw one leg in front of the other, almost falling. He could no longer see Pepe or the other man. Cameron put his other leg forward, strong yet slushy. The next moment across the courtyard felt like an eternity. When Cameron reached what was left of the stone well, he found Pepe, struck down by the rocket.

~*~

"Let's go!" screamed Alastair over the headset. Cameron suddenly realized Alastair had been screaming for a while. He lifted his head toward the copter and saw Alastair waving his arms. Nikos, his face contorted, was beside Alastair, shooting a submachine gun out into the courtyard. Across the courtyard, soldiers were running and falling. Cameron dropped his head down again to Pepe. Pepe was bloodied and half buried by heavy stone and limbs. Cameron hovered above him in an elongated moment stretching in time and pain, then dropped to his knees to shift the weight of the stones.

The intense roar of the rotors and gunfire around him faded. Smoke billowed throughout the rubble, pushed down to the ground by the rotating blades of the Dark Star, close, yet far away. Cameron realized that Alastair was kneeling down in front of Pepe.

Alastair was trying to lift Pepe. Alastair screamed at Pepe again, still all muffled, this time without the headset. Then Alastair struck Pepe. Pepe's eyes sharpened and cut into Alastair's. Pepe shook his head violently side to side. Wherever he had gone, he had now returned. He let Alastair lift him by his shoulders. Alastair pulled Pepe up from the rubble and the mutilated remnants of the Somali fighter, and then sent the large man running past Cameron.

Cameron still did not move. Real time did not return until Alastair shoved his shoulder. Sound returned to normal. He heard Alastair yell, "Let's go, let's go!" With that, Cameron turned behind Alastair and followed him to the waiting chopper.

Cameron climbed in with a liquid motion. In position, he pointed his weapon pointed out the door. As Ari began to lift the Dark Star, Cameron saw a fighter run into the courtyard from the far side of the barracks. Cameron dropped the man thoughtlessly without wasting a second round.

"Eazy, check in, this is H2," said Ari. "We have cleared the compound."

"H2, this is Eazy, do you have the package?" asked Eazy.

Ari peered over to Alastair, "We have the package."

"Bombs away," said Eazy.

Ari glanced at Alastair again. Alastair reached into his pocket and pulled out a small detonator, radio linked to the satchel of explosives Eazy had given him to leave on the first floor of the main building. With his thumb, he flipped back the safety cover then crushed the igniter. Back in the main building of the compound below, large explosions began that dwarfed all of the early detonations, and as they flew south over the beach berm the sky filled higher and higher with the aftermath of the incendiary devices.

Cameron did not watch the fireworks above the exploding compound. He found solace deep in the eyes of his brother-in-arms. Pepe, his face blackened and bloodied, held his head high, his gaze fixed on the ocean abyss, and though Cameron had no words, he felt no need to search for them. Cameron and Pepe were committed to a shared resolve. Finding Christine.

~*~

CAMERON KINCAID RETURNS IN
THE SOMALI DECEPTION
EPISODE II

~*~

ABOUT THE AUTHOR

Daniel Arthur Smith is the author of the international bestsellers *THE CATHARI TREASURE, THE SOMALI DECEPTION,* and a few other novels and short stories.

He was raised in Michigan and graduated from Western Michigan University where he studied meta-physics, cognitive science, philosophy, and comparative religion. He began his career as a bartender, barista, poetry house proprietor, teacher and then became a technologist and futurist for the Fortune 100 across the Americas and Europe.

Daniel has traveled to over 300 cities in 22 countries, residing in Los Angeles, Kalamazoo, Prague, Crete, and now writes in Manhattan where he lives with his wife and young sons.

For more information, visit **danielarthursmith.com**

STAY IN THE LOOP

Following your favorite authors on Facebook, Twitter, or other social media has become a sketchy business. Facebook and other companies block authors from conversing regularly with readers unless they are willing to cough up BIG BUX to 'promote' every post. To make sure you are receiving the latest updates, freebies, and stories on everything in the Daniel Arthur Smith universe you have to join his email newsletter. As a subscriber, you'll receive early Advance Review Copies (ARCS) of all of Daniel's books and stories... for free! In addition to all of that, Daniel regularly gives away lots of other loot like signed books and posters, so make certain that you are subscribed.

.